THE ENCHANTED WORLD OF HONEY MOON

MOUNTAIN MAYHEM

by

Suzanne Brooks Kuhn

Created by Mark Andrew Poe

Illustrations by Becky Minor
Based on the artwork of Christina Weidman

rabbit  publishers

Mountain Mayhem (The Enchanted World of Honey Moon),
by Suzanne Brooks Kuhn
Created by Mark Andrew Poe

Rabbit Publishers
1624 W. Northwest Highway
Arlington Heights, IL 60004

Illustrations by Becky Minor
Based on the artwork of Christina Weidman
Cover and Interior Design by Lewis Design & Marketing

ISBN: 978-1-943785-18-6

10 9 8 7 6 5 4 3 2 1

1. Fiction - Action and Adventure 2. Children's Fiction
First Edition
Printed in U.S.A.

The language of friendship
is not words but meanings.

— *Henry David Thoreau*

TABLE OF CONTENTS

PREFACE

Halloween visited the little town of Sleepy Hollow and never left. Many moons ago, a sly and evil mayor found the powers of darkness helpful in building Sleepy Hollow into "Spooky Town", one of the country's most celebrated attractions. Now, years later, the indomitable Honey Moon understands she must live in the town but she doesn't have to like it and she is doing everything she can to make sure that goodness and light are more important than evil and darkness.

Welcome to *The Enchanted World of Honey Moon*. Halloween may have found a home in Sleepy Hollow, but Honey and her friends are going to make sure it doesn't catch them in its Spooky Town web.

FAMILY

Honey Moon

Honey is ten-years-old. She is in the fifth grade at Sleepy Hollow Elementary School. She loves to read and she loves to spend time with her friends. Honey is sassy and spirited and doesn't have any trouble speaking her mind—even if it gets her grounded once in a while. Honey has a strong sensor when it comes to knowing right from wrong and good from evil, and like she says, when it comes to doing the right thing— Honey goes where she is needed.

Harry Moon

Harry is Honey's older brother. He is thirteen years old and in the eighth grade at Sleepy Hollow Middle School. Harry is a magician. And not just a kid magician who does kid tricks, nope, Harry has the true gift of magic.

Harvest Moon

Harvest is the baby of the Moon family. He is two-years-old. Sometimes Honey has to watch him, but she mostly doesn't mind.

Mary Moon

Mary Moon is the mom. She is fair and straightforward with her kids. She loves them dearly and they know it. Mary works full-time as a nurse, so she often relies on her family for help around the house.

John Moon

John is the dad. He's a bit of a nerd. He works as an IT professional and sometimes he thinks he would love it if his children followed in his footsteps. But he respects that Harry, Honey and possibly Harvest will need to go their own way. John owns a classic sports car he calls Emma.

Half Moon

Half Moon is the family dog. He is big and clumsy and has floppy ears. Half is pretty much your basic dog.

FRIENDS

Becky Young

Becky is Honey's best friend. They've known each other since pre-school. Becky is quiet and smart. She is an artist. She is loyal to Honey and usually lets Honey take the lead, but occasionally Becky makes her thoughts known. And she has really great ideas.

Claire Sinclair

IV

Claire is also Honey's friend. She's a bit bossy, like Honey, so they sometimes clash. Claire is an athlete. She enjoys all sports but especially soccer, softball and basketball. Sometimes kids poke fun at her rhyming name. But she doesn't mind—not one bit.

Brianna Royal

Brianna is also one of Honey's classmates. Brianna is different from all the other kids. She definitely dances to her own music. Brianna is very special. She seems to know things before they happen and always shows up in the nick of time when a friend is in trouble.

THE LONG ROAD

"Why couldn't I just take the bus like everybody else?" Honey Moon flopped forward as far as the seatbelt would allow. Her little brother, Harvest, leaned over his car seat and tried to pull the floppy, purple sun hat off her head. Honey fought to keep it on, but she pulled so hard when Harvest finally let go, Honey banged her head against the car window.

"Ouch, you made me hit my head."

Harvest giggled. But he didn't really know better.

"I would not have banged my head if I had taken the bus."

"There's no reason for you to ride with them," her dad said. He watched her in the rear-view mirror. "When we decided to take a family vacation, this seemed the logical decision."

"Great! Three hours in the mini-van with a two-year-old giving me a possible concussion is the logical decision. I'd rather be having fun with my friends." She let her head thud against the window again. "On the bus. Like I wanted."

Honey lived close enough to Sleepy

2

Hollow Elementary to walk to school, so riding the school bus was a special occasion. When her Spooky Scouts leader started planning the troop's gargantuan camping challenge, Honey had looked forward to getting to the Appalachian Trail as much as hiking it.

"And please, Honey, we don't want a repeat of last year," Mom said.

Her older brother, Harry, laughed. "I remember what happened. You couldn't make it in the woods for one night. What a bunch of girls!"

Honey glared at him over the car seat. Was it their fault it rained that day and left the ground a muddy mess? Donna, their Spooky Scout Guide, got fed up with what she called their pathetic excuses, and had called off the trip, taking them back down the trail the next morning.

None of them got their hiking patch that month. and they had to have THAT patch before they could graduate from the Mummy Mates to the Zombie Brigade. Before the

3

summer was over, Honey and her friends found out that Donna had returned to the trail, but not everyone was invited. She'd only came back with her star Mummies, those who she thought were tough enough to last.

"It's nice of them to give you a second chance," Mom said. "And now that the older girls have completed the hike, they can help you all out."

4

"And we have Donna," Honey said. Legend had it that before people had the Internet to answer all their questions, they turned to Donna. Donna was the head scoutmaster of all Sleepy Hollow. She'd earned all of her patches before she was tall enough to wade across Hawthorne Creek. She pretty much knew everything about everything.

Donna was Honey's hero and this time she wouldn't let them fail. "We have to get the patch," Honey said. "It's the last one we need. Otherwise the Jack O'Lantern Girls are going to catch us and we'll be stuck with them."

Harry laughed. "What? You don't want to be stuck with Trout singing her Spooky Scout song?" He wagged his head back and forth as he sang.

We come from Sleepy Hollow, shout it out. We are the best, there is no doubt.

It's not that we mean to flaunt, but everyone wants to be a Spooky Scout.

"I want to be Spooky Scout." Harvest waved his hands over his head. Sticky Cheerios fell off his fingers and into his hair.

"Well, I don't," Harry said. "It sounds lame to me. And Trout is a mess."

"Donna knows what she's doing," Mom said. "She and Trout make a good team."

Donna and anyone would be a good team. As for Trout...that was another story.

Trout had been a scout leader for a few years, but she'd never reached the master level. She was more suited for the younger kids...like the Jack O'Lantern Girls. She clapped and danced to the campfire songs with more energy than a grown woman ought to have. She loved crafts, but every craft she attempted ended up looking like a bird's nest. She was accident prone, allergic to everything, and had a sensitive stomach. But she smiled through all of her trials, even covered in calamine lotion.

"Take a slight left on US.... Recalculating." That was her mom's GPS on her phone. It had

a British accent because Mom had a thing for British accents. She named him Geeves.

"Recalculating?" Dad said. "I didn't make a wrong turn."

"Sometimes I think these map programs do more harm than good." Mom took the phone off its stand on the dash and tried to reset it.

"In 1.4 miles make a U-turn."

"I don't need to make a U-turn," Dad argued. "I'm going the right way."

"In 1.3 miles....Recalculating."

"Arghh...." Dad yelled. "Get the map."

There were no impatient dads on the school bus.

"The phone has the map," Harry said. "Why do you need to see it on paper?"

"Because I don't trust the phone." Dad plowed straight past the next turn around. "It doesn't know the new highway through here. It doesn't know the road construction. And when we get further out and lose the signal, then it's completely useless. An unreliable guide is the worst kind of help."

Mom pulled a map from the console and folded it down from tablecloth size to tablet. "We are on the right road. The map says it right here. I don't know what is wrong with my..."

"Uh oh," Dad said, as he slowed the van down.

Honey looked out the window. The car in the next lane had stopped. All the cars had stopped, and there were no vehicles coming toward them in the opposite lanes. A very bad sign.

"Uh oh, is right," Mom said. "This isn't good." But instead of looking out the window, Mom was studying her phone. "There's a wreck ahead. Traffic isn't moving. That's why Geeves wanted us to go a different route."

"How long is the delay?" Dad asked.

"You don't want to know," Mom answered.

Honey slid down in her seat. Great. Just great.

"Wheels on the Bus. Wheels on the Bus," Harvest chanted until Mom started the CD. As if Honey needed another reminder that she was the only one left off the bus. Her father drummed his fingers against the steering wheel.

"I'm guessing I owe Geeves an apology," he said. "I didn't think he knew what he was talking about. It sounded like bad advice at the time."

"It all depends on how much you trust your source," Mom said. "But we're in no hurry."

Maybe they weren't, but Honey was just itching to get out of the van and hit the trail with her friends.

9

✺

Two hours later they finally reached the parking lot at the entrance of Ichabod Forest. The school bus was parked next to the ranger station. Honey saw her best friend, Becky Young, sitting at a picnic table that was painted the color of rust. Claire St. Claire was slinging pinecones against the trunk of a tree hard enough to shatter them, while Brianna Royal crouched beneath an oak collecting acorns. But where were the other girls? Maybe they were still on the bus.

Dad pulled the mini-van next to the ranger station.

"I'll just get out," Honey said. "I can reach my backpack from here."

"Want out," Harvest said. "Want out."

Not only did she miss the bus ride, now her whole family was going to get out of the car and say good-bye? What a bunch of nerds. Well, maybe her friends wouldn't mind if Harry said hi. Although she knew her big brother had cooties, sometimes her friends acted weird when Harry showed up. Probably because he was a famous magician at Sleepy Hollow Middle School, but still, she wanted to go on her own.

"We don't have to get out," Mom said. "The traffic already made you late. Just lean up here and let us kiss you good-bye."

At least they weren't kissing her in front of Donna and the whole group. Honey leaned forward until Harvest's car seat was digging into her side. She tried not to look at the mashed up Cheerios in the tray as she pushed her face up in the front seat, and caught a kiss on the cheek from each parent.

"I've got something for you before you go," Dad said. He fished something shiny out of his pocket. "It's the compass, the one I showed you how to use a few weeks ago. It just might come in handy."

It wasn't any bigger than a silver dollar, but the weight of it felt good in her palm. "There's even a clip on it," she said. "I can put it on my backpack."

"You probably won't need it—Donna will keep you on track—but still it's nice to be able to figure things out for yourself."

"Thanks, Dad. Don't forget to pick me up on the other side of the mountain." Honey got out of the van.

"Be nice to the other girls," Mom said. "And be helpful. Listen to Donna."

"And don't wimp out this time," Harry said.

Honey dragged her turtle backpack off the backseat and managed to thump her older brother on the back of the head with it.

"Dad..." Harry said, but before he had time to tattle, Honey slammed the car door shut in his face. As Dad drove off, everyone waved— even Harry.

Honey watched until the car was out of sight. She took a long, deep, breath of the mountain air. Finally it was just she and nature and best friends. No little brother and no magician brother. Hiking the path was not going to be easy, but as she closed her eyes and thought of the prize at the end, she smiled. The patch. Eyes on the prize, Honey Moon. Eyes on the prize. "C'mon," she said to her dorky backpack. "Let's go! We have a job to do." She ran toward Becky.

"Honey," Becky called. "You finally made it. I was starting to worry."

"Hey, Becky." She unzipped her jacket. "Traffic jam." Now that she was away from the car's air conditioning, she felt plenty warm. "Where is everyone?" She shoved her jacket into the backpack and dropped it with the others bunched under an oak tree. She let go a deep sigh. Honey's looked out of place. Everyone else had cool, grownup-looking hiking backpacks. She was stuck using the bag she'd got for Christmas—a backpack shaped like a turtle and painted in preschool colors. At least it had enough straps and pockets on it to carry her pup tent, sleeping bag, canteen, and even a book. Honey never went anywhere without a book.

Becky smacked her gum as she answered. "Claire is busy destroying pinecones and Brianna is playing in the dirt. As for Trout..."

"I mean the other girls. Where are they?" Honey said.

Becky leaned forward and her face grew serious. "There are no other girls, Honey. Just you, me, Brianna, and Claire."

"What?" Honey looked at the long school bus and then again at the three girls outside of the ranger station. "Where are they?"

"Turns out that more of them were invited to the do-over hike than we knew. Now everyone has earned their patch except for me and you, Claire and Brianna."

15

"They all went without us?" Honey knew some of the older girls had been ready to graduate up, with or without them, but Paige and Taylor weren't any better or older than she was. It wasn't fair.

"All I need to graduate out of the Mummy Mates is this hiking patch and my friendship badge." Becky held up the camera that hung around her neck. "My project is to do a photo essay of what friendship looks like."

"Are you kidding me?" Honey said. "I'm

not worried about friendship. I'm worried about survival. How can we do this alone? We didn't even finish last time with all the big girls with us. This is a waste of time."

"What did you say?" It was Trout. The kerchief around her neck had twisted up her collar and the floppy brim of her hat was covered in fishing lures. She held a crooked walking stick with a raggedy knot of ribbons tied to the top of it. The ribbons fluttered as she sputtered. "This isn't a waste of time. We're going to have a blast. And if just one persons' life is changed this weekend, then it'd all—all the work, all the sacrifice, all the tick spray—it'd all be worth it."

Uh-oh. Trout was in her "let's give a speech" mood. Honey didn't want to hurt her feelings. She just wanted to start walking so they could get to the north ranger station and earn the patch. Her sash had a blank spot on it. A patch—that was all she was after.

"It won't be a waste," Honey said, "if we succeed and get our patches."

Trout fiddled with one of the lures on her hat. "And we will succeed. Usually if I'm going to fail, I would've already hurt myself— Ouch!" A lure had stabbed her in the finger. Trout jerked her hand away, but the hat was firmly

17

attached. The strap beneath her chin caught and jerked her head downward. Trout, in complete panic mode, beat her hand against her hat. "It's got me. Get it off. Get it off."

That was when Claire came running toward them. "What's wrong?" she called.

"Trout caught her finger on a fishing hook," Honey said.

Becky took Trout by the wrist to stop the thrashing. "Here, let me look."

18

"I'm going to get Donna," Honey said, but Claire stopped her.

"Donna isn't here."

Honey froze. Claire's face reflected the terror that Honey felt. No Donna?

"Where is she?"

"She didn't come," Claire said. "She and the Zombie Brigade girls had a Spooky Scouts awards ceremony at the capital. That's where they are."

Honey felt butterflies flutter in her stomach. She looked around the empty parking lot. "You mean we're going on a hike without Donna? We're going into the wild with Trout? And only Trout?"

Trout tried to look up, but since her hat was pinned to her finger, the brim still covered her face.

"Hey, I'm right here," she said.

"Be still," Becky said. "I'm having trouble getting this out."

"I have a pocket knife." Claire unzipped her backpack.

"No knife, Claire," Trout hollered. She swung her hand away from Becky and the hat.

"Finally free," Becky said. "With half my finger gone."

"You shouldn't have hooked it on your hat," Becky answered.

"First aid kit," Trout said. "I need a band-aid. I think there's one on the bus."

"Shouldn't we have the first aid kit with us?" Honey asked. Without Donna, and only Trout in charge, Honey knew it was up to her, Becky, and Claire to see this hike to the finish. Brianna tended to wander away on field trips. So Honey knew she'd have to watch out for her, especially.

Honey should've told her parents how much she loved them before they'd said good-bye.

HITTING THE TRAIL

Trout punched her fist in the air as if a stadium of fans would erupt with cheers. "Time to hit the trail."

Honey looked at the dark woods. There

could be some scary stuff up ahead, but she was determined to get that Hiking Patch. She was not about to let some creepy old spiders and worms and rain stop her this time. But just as she was about to take a step toward the trail, Claire grabbed her by the shoulder. "We have to talk."

"Okay, okay," Honey said. "What gives?"

"Look," Claire said.

They watched Becky help Trout with her backpack. "You have your pack on upside down. Everything will fall out," Becky said.

Claire dragged her away from the others. "What are we going to do?" She shook Honey so that her sun hat wobbled. "She's loony," Claire said. "We'd stand a better chance all by ourselves."

"Maybe. But that's not how it works. We just have to keep our eye on Trout and hope we don't get lost or . . . or worse!" Honey spotted Brianna standing alone near the tallest pine tree she had ever seen. "And then there's Brianna. We should keep an eye out for her too."

Claire nodded. "Okay. Look at her. Is she going for a Pocahontas look?"

Brianna had threaded feathers into her long blond braids, although that didn't make her look like any Indian princess Honey had ever seen. Especially not with the added touch of a safari hat.

23

Briana walked a few steps toward Honey and Claire and shook her head. "I hope Trout knows when to go up the mountain and when to go down," she said.

Claire groaned. "This is trouble. Trout can't help us and Becky isn't really much of an outdoors person."

"She likes flowers and cuddly animals," Honey said. "But I don't think camping is her thing."

"No offense, Brianna," Claire said. "But

someone's going to have to keep an eye on you all the time to make sure you don't wander off and get lost. Remember the Mayflower?"

"I'm not going to get lost this time." Brianna stood on her tippy toes in her leather moccasins. "I promised my mom I would always be able to see one of you. I have two eyes and three friends, so I have a friend to spare even."

24

Brianna had trouble staying focused. Becky liked everything neat and organized. Dirt, sweat, and germs weren't her thing. And Claire had a knack for losing her temper and making people mad. What a team.

Honey wasn't about to go home without at least trying.

"We need our patch. We can't get further behind or we won't be able to promote to the Zombies, and then we'll never reach Tombstone Teens before high school. We've got to do this, Claire. It's you and me."

If there was one thing that Honey could usually count on, it was Claire's winner-take-all competitiveness.

"C'mon, girls!" Trout thumped her walking stick against the ground. "Let's do this."

Honey, Claire, and Brianna joined them. "Is everyone ready?" Becky asked.

"Do you have the first aid kit?" Honey asked Trout.

Trout nodded, the fishing lures waving from her brim. "Check!"

"Do you have..." Honey caught sight of Brianna, struggling to carry a loaded backpack. "Wait a minute. What all have you packed?"

No one would be surprised to hear Brianna had something unusual in her backpack. She was the queen of the unexpected. But the amount of gear she had pinned, tied and strapped to her backpack was astounding.

"I just brought stuff I thought we'd need. Like a roll of toilet paper, a dust pan, and hand broom to clean out our tents, a *Spooky Scouts* flag to hang over our campground at night, and my pair of furry, sparkly house-shoe boots."

"How much does that weigh?" Becky asked. "Aren't you worried about it being too heavy?"

"It's all stuff we might need." Brianna pouted. "A Spooky Scout is always prepared."

Even Trout seemed to think it was a bad idea. "You have to keep up with the team. If your backpack gets too heavy, we'll have to leave stuff behind, and I'm sure your mom wouldn't want that."

"Don't worry," Brianna said. "I promised my mom I wouldn't get lost this time. I'm sticking to you closer than the lures stick to Trout's fingers." Brianna bent over, picked up an acorn and stuck it in her pocket. "I'm saving them so I can feed the squirrels."

Oh no. This was not the time for Brianna's mind to wander away to Planet Space Brianna. They'd never get her attention again.

"I say we let her carry it," Becky said. "She never complains."

True. Brianna followed her own music, but she never complained about the consequences. Besides, she wasn't Honey's responsibility.

"Every man for himself." Claire spun her baseball hat around backwards.

"Or in this case, every Mummy Mate for herself," Honey said.

Trout looked up at the sun, then down at her phone. "Enough chin-wagging. We're late to the race. Time to go-go-go." With her head down she took long strides across the parking lot to the rangers' station.

"Ummm," Becky raised her hand. "Excuse me, Trout. Isn't the beginning of the trail here?" Becky pointed at the wooden sign that had the words *Perdition Path* burned into it.

Trout squinted at the sign. She pulled a map out of her pocket and turned it this way and that, trying to find the top.

"Just like her backpack," Brianna said.

Honey, Claire and Becky shared a worried glance.

"Gold star for you, Becky Young," Trout said. "That is the right way. Okey-dokey. Let's go." Her knotty, wooden staff thudded against the ground as she marched off just as confidently as before, but in the right direction this time.

"We're never going to make it," Becky whispered to Honey.

"We have to," Honey said. "We could do it by ourselves."

29

"No, we couldn't. Remember last year? And we even had Donna."

Honey had thought the same thing, but she didn't like hearing it from Becky. Becky was supposed to be the encourager. Becky was the optimist. Honey was too smart to think everything would turn out all right every time.

"Hey, guys." Claire caught up with them.

"Are you ready for tomorrow?"

Tomorrow? Wasn't surviving today enough? Honey wasn't worried about tomorrow yet.

"What's special about tomorrow?" Becky asked.

"Oh, I don't know," Claire said. "I just think it's going to be a great day."

30   Honey was worried about Claire. Had she already caught some nasty disease from an optimistic parasite? She wasn't acting like herself.

"Girls. Keep up," Trout called. "We have to reach the end of the trail by noon on Sunday or else we failed. The Spooky Scouts don't award badges for tardiness."

Their backpacks creaked and jingled with every step. Brianna kept up, but walked a little behind them singing *Bingo was His Name-O*. She picked up a feather from the ground and added it to her braid.

"Do you think we'll make the campsite before dark?" Becky asked. "We got a late start." Honey looked up through the leaves above her at the sun, which had already started on its way back down. "We need to speed up," she said. "Last year we left earlier and still barely had time to get our tents up before dark."

Brianna stopped singing. "Are you worried about the dark? I brought something for you. Let's stop." She slid her backpack off her shoulders. It smashed onto the ground like a boulder, kicking up a small cloud of dust and dead leaves.

As Brianna unfastened a side pocket, Honey looked up the trail. Trout was just about to disappear behind a thick stand of evergreens.

"Trout," Honey called. "Wait for us."

Trout turned and hurried back. "Did you find something? Let me see. Let me see." But before she could get back, Trout suddenly stopped and dropped to her knees. "Wow!" she said. "Would you look at that?" She shrugged off her backpack, yanked open the front pouch and pulled out a small, thin book.

"Now what?" Honey said.

"We better go see," Becky said.

Even Brianna forgot about her surprise and followed Honey, Claire, and Becky.

32

Trout flipped through the pages of the colorful book. "Here it is. On page thirteen. See this picture? Then look down there." She pointed to a dark pile beneath the tree. "I'm not one hundred percent sure, but I think that's raccoon scat."

Becky and Claire jumped back. "Ewww...," they cried.

"You have a book about poop? Cool," Honey said.

"This book is a very helpful guide to learning about the animals we are sharing the woods with. It's nice to know what's walking around out here with us."

"Sure," Honey said. "We can use all the info we can get."

Claire laughed "At least it's not scratch and sniff."

"Doesn't anyone want to see what I brought?" Brianna had returned to her over-sized backpack.

33

"We're sorry," Becky said. "What did you bring?"

"Please don't tell me that she has poop in her bag." Claire shook her head at their loopy leader, as Trout wandered off with her book looking for more samples to match.

"I didn't bring poop," Brianna said. "I brought a flashlight for everyone."

"Flashlights were on the packing list," Honey said. "We each have one already."

"But not like these. They are short and they stick on your hat with a magnet. See?" She took off her safari hat and placed a round piece of metal inside of it. Holding the metal in just the right spot, she attached the glass bulb to the other side. The two sides snapped together by the force of the magnet.

"It looks like the kind of lights miners wear," Claire said.

34

"Yes," Brianna said. "Look." With a touch, the light shone weakly in the shadow of the pines. "When it gets dark the light will help illuminate the path." Brianna pulled herself up to her full height. Honey thought she looked very proud.

"That's really smart," Honey said. And if there was anything she liked, it was when people made smart choices. "Then we have our hands free."

Brianna beamed as bright as her hat. "I thought it would come in handy setting up our tents too. Especially if we don't get there until dark."

"You are so thoughtful." Becky adjusted her light to get it into the perfect place. She held her hat away from her to judge how it looked. "We each have our own little sun beam."

Claire had already fastened hers onto her baseball cap. "This would be great for late night pick-up games when the lights at the park are out." She smiled at Brianna. "Good thinking."

With a grunt, Brianna picked up her bag and slung it over her shoulder. "A Spooky Scout is always prepared."

"Have you seen Trout?" Becky turned a full circle, then her gaze followed the straight tree trunks up to the sky. "She was here just a minute ago. Where could she have gone?"

"We don't have time to waste," Claire said. "Let's go."

Honey looked up the path. Trout had disappeared. "Oh nooo. Come on. We better catch up with our fearless leader before it's too late."

PILGRIM'S PROGRESS

"I'll go this way." Becky said

"No." Honey grabbed her by the sleeve of her rainbow jacket. "We can't split up. That's the number one rule of hiking. Stay together.

Buddy system and all that."

"We didn't split up," Brianna said. "Trout did."

"I think it would be best if we waited here until she comes back," Honey said.

"Probably found some new poop to investigate." Claire swatted at a gnat.

Brianna gasped. "Do you have bugs? Well, guess what I brought? Bug spray." She dropped her backpack on the ground again and rolled it over until she found the correct pocket. She handed Claire a pump bottle decorated with flowers and vines. "It's all natural. Smells good even."

Claire sprayed it on her shoulders. "Good enough for now, but I brought the killer stuff. It's one hundred percent DEET, or something like that. Bugs vaporize on contact."

Overkill. That was Claire.

"Come to think of it," said Honey, "Trout

38

got lost a few times on the trail last year. Remember that? We ate lunch without her, then found her waiting for us at the next creek crossing."

Claire tossed the bug spray back to Brianna. "Let's get going, then. No use waiting around here."

"I have a map." Honey pulled the folded paper out of her pocket and spread it on a tree trunk. "We haven't gone far. Here we are. When the trail finally forks, we go left."

"I bet Trout will be waiting for us there," Becky said. "Maybe she just wants to see if we can make it on our own."

Honey doubted that Trout had planned a challenge for them. She'd probably forgotten about them altogether. In that case, it was up to Honey to take charge.

"Let's stop wasting time," Honey said. "Forward march!"

The girls set out over the leaf-littered ground. The sun dappled the trail in front of them, making bright yellow spots of light on the ground. Smells of damp dirt and cedar seemed to clear Honey's lungs and make her eyes clearer. Claire and Becky walked ahead of her, shoulder-to-shoulder, laughing about something they'd seen on the bus ride there, but Honey enjoyed the solitude. Birdsong trilled through the woods. At first she tried to identify each one, but finally gave up and just listened.

It could be said Honey spent too much time reading books, but reading books helped her appreciate the beauty of nature and made her expect to see something important. And so when a cardinal landed in front of her, and hopped around a bit, she held her breath, hoping to see Emily Dickinson's poem played out in real life:

A bird came down the walk.
He did not know I saw.
He bit an angle-worm in halves
And ate the fellow, raw.
And then he drank a dew

From a convenient grass,
And then hopped sidewise to the wall
To let a beetle pass.

But there was no beetle. Not even a worm. Still, Honey might write her own poem about the pretty brown cardinal (brown because it was a girl) with the bright orange beak and the jagged crest on top of its head. In her poem, the bird would be on a mission to fly to the highest tree and to get there before noon on Sunday. That's what Honey's poem would be about.

41

They were going to conquer this trail, once and for all.

Honey looked behind her to check on the other girls. Claire and Becky kept the quick pace with her, but it seemed Brianna had drifted further and further away but still in sight.

"Hey, guys. Wait for Brianna."

Becky and Claire stopped. Brianna walked

up the hill. "Thanks, Honey. This backpack is heavier than I thought."

How could she not predict that giant bag would've been too heavy? It was the size of the bean bags in the school library.

"We can walk slower," Becky said.

"No we can't," Claire said. "We have to make it to the campsite."

42

"I think we're almost to the fork in the road." Honey rustled the map around so she could check. "I bet Trout will be there waiting for us."

"Yoo-hoo."

They all turned at once. Trout was trudging up the trail behind them. "You were going at a good pace," she said. "I was trying to catch you all this time, but you kept going faster and faster."

"We thought you were ahead of us," Honey said. "We were trying to catch you."

"A dog chasing its tail." Trout laughed. "But now we're all together again. Does anyone need a drink?"

"I've been keeping hydrated." Claire held up her bottle of blue sports drink.

"Does anyone need to go potty?" Trout asked.

"Nope." Honey was afraid that Trout would pull out her book and try to identify it.

"Then, let's carry on." Trout cheered and started ahead with her staff tapping the way.

The girls clustered up as they started moving.

"Do you think she's mad we didn't wait for her?" Becky asked.

44 Becky always worried about other people's feelings. "She's fine," Honey said. "Just think of all the ground we've covered." But she looked again at the map and saw that they had a long way to go before they could rest. She put it back in her pocket with the compass her dad had given her. She knew she'd need the map again, especially with Trout in the lead.

"Today is the last day that...." Claire paused and seemed to be looking somewhere far away for a few seconds. "The last day that something is going to be the way it is, but you all already know that. It's a nice day, but not as great as tomorrow will be."

Honey wrinkled her nose. What was wrong with Claire? The only way she'd notice the weather was if her softball game was going to be rained out. It wasn't like her to appreciate beauty in anything other than a perfect jump shot.

"There are clouds coming in," Honey said. "And the wind is kicking up a little. If it rains..."

"I'm not worried about that," Claire said. "I mean... I just mean, don't you think this weekend is important?"

"Sure. We're going to finally earn our patches," Honey said. "If that's what you're talking about."

Claire rolled her eyes. "Never mind. I bet Becky gets it, but you obviously don't."

Honey got the beauty of their surroundings, but she didn't get why Claire cared suddenly.

They reached the crest of a hill just as the gusts hit them full force.

"Wow," Trout said. "There is a storm coming in after all. I thought the weather reports were exaggerating."

"You knew a storm was coming?" Honey rested her hand on her hip.

"A little rain doesn't hurt anyone," Trout said. "We'll be snug as bugs in our tents by the time the rain starts to fall."

Brianna tilted her head up and sniffed. "She's right," she said. "Smells like rain. But, don't worry, it won't be here for another couple of hours."

Honey motioned her troops closer. "A couple of hours? We need to get to the campground, find firewood, cook dinner and get our tents set up in that time. Now look..." She pulled the map out from her pocket. "Here's where we are. We won't make it to the camp and get all that done by then."

Trout scratched her neck. "You think we're there? I thought we were further." She took the map and turned it upside down. "See. We're going this direction."

And that is exactly why Honey's dad gave her a compass. With a flourish, she pulled it out of her pocket and held it out before her. She adjusted her stance until the arrow pointed north. She raised an eyebrow at Trout, who tucked a strand of graying hair behind her ear and turned the map the correct way.

"Honey is right. We aren't even close. We're going to have to hunker down somewhere around here."

"It's not dark yet," Claire said.

"But it will be soon and we want to have our camp set before the rain starts," Trout said.

"We don't want to be on top of a hill during a storm," Honey said. "That's a lightning danger."

All eyes looked to Trout for affirmation. "We'll head that way." Trout pointed to a steep, gravel gully. "That looks like the fastest way down the mountain. We can follow the creek around the mountain in the morning and pick up where we left off."

"Sounds good," Claire said. "Let's hoof it."

"Downhill, finally," Becky said.

"Yes!" Brianna cheered.

48

Carefully, they braced themselves against the trees and inched their way down. Gravel rolled, causing Honey to skid a few feet at a time. She didn't take a step without holding onto a tree trunk, or else she might just fall the rest of the way with nothing to stop her. Becky and Claire were in front of her, so when she stepped in a pile of loose gravel, her heel slid forward, causing her to fall on her bottom and kick Claire.

Claire lunged for the nearest tree and hugged it like it was her first time on a skateboard. "What are you trying to do? Kill me?"

"Sorry," Honey said. "I lost my balance." She

pulled herself up and dusted off her caboose. "I'll be more careful."

"Timber!"

"Who said that?" Honey spun around. Her feet slipped but she managed to grab onto a week sapling and regain her balance.

"It was Brianna," Becky called. "Look."

Honey watched Brianna's giant backpack tumble down the hill right at her.

"Duck!" Brianna yelled, as she hit the ground.

With a hand around a sapling and her face in the gravel, the backpack tumbled past Honey.

Claire dove into a shrub while Becky grabbed Trout by the arm and dragged her out of the way.

Branches cracked and pebbles flew as the backpack crashed down the hill. The three girls and their leader watched in stunned silence until it reached the bottom far below.

"Whoo-hoo!" Brianna cheered.

Honey scrambled to her feet. "You could've killed us."

"No, I aimed it just right. And now..." she walked past them on the steep hill. "...now I don't have to carry my heavy backpack."

Claire and Becky exchanged looks. Honey kind of appreciated Brianna's clever use of gravity. Tossing her backpack took no effort and just look how far her equipment had gone. That sort of creative thinking made Brianna a genius—sometimes. Sometimes it just made for a disaster.

But at least they weren't waiting on Brianna anymore. Without a backpack weighing her down, she cruised down the hill like an Olympic skier, while Honey and the rest of the troop watched.

"She's a spitfire," shouted Trout. "Watch her go. Go! GO!"

All Honey could do was shake her head.

"Come on down," Brianna called up at them. "There's a creek. It's so pretty."

"Hi Ho, Hi Ho, girls," shouted Trout. "Let's hit the gravely trail."

They soon broke out of the trees and walked out on the rocky creek bank.

"Wow," Honey said. "That was kind of exciting." She looked back up the hill.

"I'll say," Becky said.

The creek gurgled and bubbled. Everyone shed their backpacks with sighs of relief. Claire and Brianna waded waist deep into the crystal clear water. Becky took the lens cap off her camera and snapped pictures of them splashing. Honey sat down on a warm rock at the edge, pulled her shoes off and shook the gravel out of them. "Geeze," she said. "I must have picked up a pound of dirt."

Honey noticed Trout standing there with her hands on her hips surveying the area.

"Whatcha doing?" Honey called as she retied her laces.

"We don't want to be too close to the

river," Trout said. "But there aren't many clearings around here. Not enough room for a campfire and our tents with all the trees."

No, a campfire wouldn't be a great idea there with the pine needles and the dead leaves. Honey decided to look for a possible campsite herself. Maybe there'd be a place like this, but further away from the river. She took off through the trees, always keeping the creek in view so she could find her way back. She found the perfect place for their camp. But she'd investigate before she bragged to the others. She hated being wrong.

Just like the path they'd come down on, this was a clear, dry area, well above the creek. It slanted down, but not steep enough to lose anyone in the night. The barren, sandy area was wide enough that they could build a nice-sized campfire without being in danger of catching the forest on fire. In fact, they could gather their tents around it for warmth and light.

It was perfect, and now she could brag.

"I found it." Honey walked back to the valley. "I found the best place. It's high enough to be safe from the creek, but low enough that we won't be in danger of lightning. It has a great place for a fire and no rocks, so it'll be soft to sleep on."

Trout nodded and slung her backpack over her shoulder. "Load up, girls. Honey is leading the way."

54

FOOD FAIL

Honey took off with a spring in her step. She liked leading the way. She liked being the one who found the solutions to problems. She liked impressing people. And her friends would be impressed, no doubt about it.

She stopped at the edge of the sandy ravine and presented it to the Mummy Mates with a grandiose wave of her arm. "Here it is. The perfect camp site."

"This is it?" Claire trudged ahead a few steps. "I don't want to get sand in my sleeping bag."

"It's not very pretty." Becky twirled her curly ponytail around her finger. "There aren't many trees."

"And there's no shelter from the rain." Brianna took a bite of a jumbo, chocolatron bar.

Honey didn't let on that she felt like she had been punched in the stomach. "First off," she said with a smidgen of annoyance. "We have to sleep on the ground anyway, Claire. Sand will be much more comfortable than rocks or tree roots, plus it'll be really easy to hammer our tent stakes into."

Claire looked at her feet.

"And Becky," Honey continued. "You can't see how pretty it is in the dark, so what's the big deal?"

"I'm sorry," Brianna said as she chewed.

"Thanks," Honey said. "But trees aren't going to keep us dry. Plus, don't forget they are a lightning hazard." She looked around at the small troop. "Anything else?"

Trout put her arm around Honey's shoulders. "Don't worry, Honey. It's a grand spot. This is the best place to sleep in the whole forest, I'm sure."

But that only made Honey feel even more pathetic.

"Well, are we staying here, or not?" Honey asked.

"Sure, why not?" Claire said. She dropped her backpack first. Then Becky dropped hers, and then Brianna. Her backpack landed with a loud thud. Honey laughed. "Now we're camping," she said.

They each opened the drawstring bag that held their pup tents. Honey's dad had taught her how to put hers up in the backyard. He didn't like this model because the spikes weren't very strong, but in this soft soil, Honey could push them in with her hand. She liked them a lot.

58

Honey unrolled her tent on the sand, but she noticed Becky doing something strange. Becky was on her knees. She moved her hand along the sandy ground making a hollow about the size of her body, Honey figured. Every time her finger brushed against a pebble, she dug it up and tossed it aside. Leave it to Becky to know how to make a campsite more comfortable. Honey followed her lead until she'd smoothed an area big enough for her bed. Then, once the small, green tent was up, Honey pulled her sleeping bag out of her turtle backpack and tossed it into the tent.

It was getting dark. Not dark enough for a flashlight yet, but she had one on her head, so why not? Honey switched the thing on. She looked toward Becky. Becky's smile reflected back at her. Becky switched her headlamp on and soon they were all shooting beams of light at each other. Except Brianna, who was still wrestling with her tent.

"Let's help," Honey said.

"Thanks," Brianna said. "I'm not very good at these things."

"It's easier with two people," Becky said.

"Good job, girls. And Honey, thank you for noticing a fellow scout in need and doing something about it. Good friendship skills," Trout commented.

Honey smiled. "Thanks, what's next?"

"We need firewood," she answered. "Let's get a stack started right here in the middle of the camp itself."

"All right," Honey said. But just as she said the words, a gust of wind whipped through the campsite. She wrestled her tent flap to get it fastened down.

Collecting firewood without an ax pretty much left you at the mercy of the weather casualties and of carpenter ants that killed a tree, or at the very least, a branch.

The first downed branch she found was a lot lighter than it looked, but still awkwardly long. She propped it against another trunk and stomped her foot through it. It crumpled like a twig. "No problem," Honey said.

She tossed the broken pieces aside. "Now for the next one." She picked up another branch, which was considerably heavier, although no bigger. She'd show these sticks who was boss. Honey again lifted her foot, but this time, no matter how hard she stomped, the branch wouldn't crack. Her knee bounced back up, nearly hitting her in the chest. Fire shot through her ankle as she fell backwards and landed on her rump.

"Oww..." She held her ankle in both hands and glared at the limb that remained propped against the tree, mocking her. She wouldn't give in. That branch will break. But when she stood up, pain shot all the way up to the enamel on her teeth. There'd be no stomping on boards for the rest of the night.

Feeling like a sissy, Honey limped in circles, gathering all the smaller twigs that didn't need a karate chop to break. It'd be enough to get the fire started at least.

61

By the time she made it back to camp, her ankle felt better. Pride surged through her at the sight of the troop tents arranged so orderly. Brianna had even hung the Mummy Mates flag from a tree branch at the edge of the clearing. They could do this. Even without the older girls and Donna, they could finish this challenge and earn their patches.

Honey limped to the center of the camp and dumped her sticks there. Brianna had already started digging in the sand to make a fire pit. Becky carried an armful of pine cones for kindling.

"Why are you limping?" Becky asked.

"Oh, it's okay. Just a minor sprain. I'm fine." She rubbed her stomach. "But I won't be if we don't eat soon."

"Yeah, I'm hungry," Becky said.

Honey's headlight beamed on Trout as she was staking the last corner of her tent. It looked brand-new with a picture of a hiking man on the corner. The picture showed that the tent had a little flap that she could prop up with poles to make a shady "porch".

Trout pulled the stake tight and shoved it into the sandy soil.

"Wow," Honey said. "Your tent is tight. Maybe I need to do mine better."

Trout's tent was pulled so tight the floor didn't touch the ground beneath it.

"Yeah, you don't want there to be any slack," Trout said. She opened the zipper to her tent and tossed her backpack inside.

Kerplunk! Honey's eyes widened as each corner of the tent ripped out of the sand and the floor of the tent sagged to the ground.

Trout shook her head. "Here I was so happy that the stakes went in so easily. Easy come, easy go, I guess."

Honey took a step backwards. "It's not too bad. You can stick the stakes in again."

Claire came out of the trees with more firewood. She could do real karate kicks without twisting her ankle. She added her armful to Honey's.

"What's for dinner?" Claire asked.

Trout, who was still staring at her tent said, "I brought hot dogs, a can of beans and stuff for s'mores. It'll be amazing." Trout pulled the stake tight and shoved it back into the sandy soil.

"Trout?" Honey said. "Where are the hot dogs?"

"In the cooler."

Honey looked around her. She didn't see a cooler. Unless there was a cooler inside Trout's backpack.

"Oh, the cooler!" Trout slapped herself on the forehead. "I left it at the ranger station. I'll go back and get it."

"No." Honey grabbed her sleeve. "You can't leave. It took us all afternoon to get here and it's already dark."

"You forgot the food?" Claire sat on the pile of firewood. "Just great! This is the Worst. Day. Ever! I should be home eating... eating..." She looked around at the group of girls. "Oh, never mind!"

"Does anyone know how to set traps?" Honey asked. "Or how about fishing? Trout has lures on her hat."

"Let's just throw her hat in the river and see what we catch." Claire was cranky when everything was going her way. Get her hungry and she was vicious.

"I don't want to kill any animals." Becky twisted her hands. "We'd have to cut them up and cook them and... well, I'm sure it isn't healthy."

"I have food."

Everyone turned to look at Brianna. She grabbed her backpack by the strap and dragged it over the rocks to them. "I brought enough food for everyone."

65

"Hallelujah!" Claire cried. "What do you have?"

"Let's see." Brianna unzipped another of the many pockets and began pulling groceries out. "There's peanut butter, ketchup, three boxes of mac-n-cheese, and tortillas."

Honey closed her eyes before she said something mean. What in the world were they supposed to do with that? Did Brianna pack for a trip, or just throw random food in her bag?

Brianna lined up the food on a flat rock. "I packed everything that sounded delicious. I love mac-n-cheese. Peanut butter sandwiches are my favorite, and I figured we'd be having hot dogs so I didn't want to forget the ketchup. The tortillas...I forgot about them. They might have been in the backpack since last year."

"Ewww...." They groaned in unison.

But Honey was already making plans. "We can cook mac-n-cheese on the fire. We have water at the river. We just need...." She looked around. "Did anyone bring a pot?"

"I did," Trout said. "But I left that on the bus."

"Or we could boil water in a tin can," Claire said. "We learned that last year."

"Does anyone one have a tin can?" Honey asked.

"I do," Trout said.

"Don't tell me," Claire said. "It's in the bus."

"Now that you mention it..."

"We all have trail mix," Becky said. "But that won't last us. We should save that for tomorrow."

Definitely. What if they got lost? They couldn't

cut into their emergency supplies yet. So depending on the tortillas, it looked like peanut butter was the only edible thing available. And dry mac-n-cheese.

Honey took the cardboard mac and cheese box and ripped the lid off. Then she opened the jar of peanut butter and scooped a tiny amount out on the crescent of macaroni. She popped it into her mouth and chewed the crunchy snack. It tasted like—well, like peanut butter and dry macaroni, which wasn't bad, even if it did hurt her teeth.

"You have to have protein," Trout said. "So all in all, this is a very nutritious meal."

Claire shrugged past them and reached for the tortillas. She squirted a line of ketchup down the middle, rolled it up and ripped off a big bite. "Don't look at me weird," she said. "You're the ones eating macaroni bones."

"I can't eat that," Becky said. "It'd be too much like eating fingernail clippings." She lifted the packet of powdered cheese out of the box and looked at her water bottle. "Do you think I could make cheese with water? It might be worth a try."

"And pour it on the dry macaroni?" Honey shook her head. "The peanut butter is better."

Trout beamed. "I am so proud of you girls. This is what real survival is all about. Taking the materials at hand and putting them to good use."

Honey thought survival was about being prepared and not leaving all the food in the bus, but what did she know?

Eating peanut butter mac-n-cheese one at a time was no way to get full. Honey licked her fingers when she was done. Two boxes left and plenty of peanut butter. "What's for breakfast?" she asked.

"I have packets of instant oatmeal, and fruit, too," said Trout.

"On the bus?" Claire asked.

Her smile faded. "Yeah, it's on the bus."

"Don't worry," Brianna said. "I can find something else in here, I'm sure."

"I hope she brought powdered donuts." said Becky, who had been sitting criss-cross apple-sauce, stretched her feet out in front of her. She pushed the pile of branches. They'd never got around to lighting the fire, and now it was dark. "I love powdered donuts." The talk turned to their favorite meals, which only made Honey miss her family. They were probably eating at Tiny's Pizza World right now, with the buffet that had over one hundred items on it and all the ice cream you could eat. She'd started to get sad when the first drops of rain fell.

"Everyone to your tents," Trout said. "We don't want to get wet. See you in the morning."

MIDNIGHT SWIM

At first the rain just pattered lightly on Honey's tent. It was a soft, fun sound that made her drowsy. She wiggled her feet in the bottom of her sleeping bag, pushing the sand around in patterns through the floor of her tent. Snug as a bug in a rug. The waterproof tent meant that she could enjoy the sound of the storm without worrying about getting wet.

She fell asleep quickly, but the occasional lightning flash or roll of thunder woke her. The drive to the park and the long hike had exhausted her, and what would've normally made her worry, only caused her to open her

72

eyes, then to drowse back to sleep.

She dreamed she was floating down the river. Safe and secure. Trees fell and splashed into the river. The wind howled and lightning crackled, but nothing could touch Honey Moon. Peacefully, she rocked along, just like Moses in the bullrushes, except she drifted in an inner tube. Or maybe it was a floating raft. She wasn't quite sure because the dream kept changing. Once she dangled her hand over the edge of the raft and her hand got wet. Once she thought her backside was in the cold water— that was the dream with the inner tube—but she still slept on, rocking gently in the midst of the storm until she heard her name called.

"Honey! Honey get up." She raised her hand out of the water and waved. Couldn't they see she was taking a nap? The river was peaceful. Why couldn't they leave her alone?

"Honey!"

A gust of wind tore through the camp and suddenly she wasn't sleeping anymore. She was

73

in her tent and her tent was falling over her face. Wet canvas covered her mouth and nose. Gasping, she pushed her hands over her head to take a breath. The wind howled, plastering the roof of her tent to her head. She rolled over in her sleeping bag into a puddle. It was a moving puddle, streaming beneath the floor of her tent.

She felt like she was inside a giant, wet, deflated balloon. She felt around for the tent door. Cold metal met her fingers. The zipper! She yanked it open. The water was rising fast.

Behind the flashlight that was blinding her, she heard Trout's voice. "Drag your tent and stuff to higher ground. It's a flash flood."

The sand around Honey's tent stakes had all washed away, leaving only gaps in the dirt. Honey grabbed the soggy corner of her tent and dragged it up to the trees and out of the growing stream that raced down the mountain.

Trout was at Claire's tent, but Honey couldn't see Becky and Brianna. The lightning flashed and Honey could see thick streams of water coursing through their campground, pushing the sand away to draw deep rivulets in the ground. Honey dropped her tent and dashed to Becky's tent. The stakes that were supposed to hold it secure floated aimlessly. Only Becky's weight was holding the sleeping bag in place.

Honey threw open the tent flap. "Becky. Becky." Honey grabbed the foot of Becky's sleeping bag. With a lunge, Honey pulled the sleeping bag a foot.

75

"Becky, get up. You're sleeping in a river!" At least her tent hadn't fallen down. Honey felt for her hat with the flashlight, but it wasn't there. Honey knew Becky was a deep sleeper, but this was ridiculous. At slumber parties they could decorate her whole face with lipstick and shaving cream and she wouldn't wake up. Drastic measures were required.

With both hands, Honey grabbed Becky's foot through the sleeping bag and started walking backwards. The sleeping bag hung up for a moment at the tent opening, then slipped past. The rain pounded Becky's face. She tried to slink into the sleeping bag and hide. Honey looked up to see Trout and Claire helping Brianna move her giant backpack up the hill. The rain and wind kept a steady pace, but the water coming down the gully was getting higher. And Becky was only now starting to wake up.

"Why, Honey?" She rubbed the rain off her face. "Let me sleep."

"You're going to be sleeping with the fishes if you don't wake up," Honey said. "We need to save your tent."

Finally, Becky started getting herself together. She winced as her bare feet hit the water. She picked up her sleeping bag and stumbled her way to the trees. Honey grabbed Becky's pillow and backpack out of the water, and then joined the rest of the troop huddled beneath a thick maple tree.

They stood in shocked silence, shivering and watching the fast water racing to the bottom of the hill.

Honey's heart sank into her boots. She fought back tears. "I thought this would be a good dry place, because there were no rocks or trees." She sniffed. "But I think we set up our camp in a dry creek bed."

"Brilliant." Claire hugged a teddy bear that Honey had never seen before. Claire glared at Honey, and then stuffed the teddy bear into her backpack.

"Did we save everything?" Brianna asked.

"I think so," Brianna said. "Is anything dry?"

Becky fell to her knees to unfasten her camera bag. "Please, please, please," she said as she fumbled with the snaps. Then she triumphantly drew out the small square camera. "Look! It's still dry!" She held it to her face and pushed the button.

The light flashed.

Honey's eyes were seared with a blinking red square that floated in front of whatever she was trying to look at.

"I'm blind." Trout said. "No more flashes."

"Sorry." Becky snapped the lens cap back on. "I'm going to carry this in my bag now, or it'll get wet in the rain." She unzipped her backpack and groaned. "Oh no. Everything is soaked."

They all looked at the sorry, wet heap of clothes she had in her hand. Their tents, their backpacks and their sleeping bags had all gotten wet from the stream. But now even their clothes were drenched.

"We are definitely earning our patches," Honey said. "Just think of the poor Continental Soldiers with George Washington at Valley Forge." They had it a lot worse. At least it wasn't cold. And no one was shooting musket balls at them.

"Yet," Claire said.

Everyone let go a nervous laugh.

"Are we going to just sit here under a tree all night?" Claire shivered. "I think that's child abuse."

Uh-oh. They'd talked Trout and Donna into ending their hike last year at this precise moment. It had been late at night and everyone was tired and discouraged. That's when they'd given up and headed back to the bus. Honey had to stop Claire from calling it quits. They didn't want to ruin another year's worth of work and have to repeat the Mummy Mates because of a moment's weakness.

"This isn't that bad," Honey said. "It's just rain. We'll dry out as soon as the sun comes up."

"And how long is that?"

They both turned to Trout. Trout pulled her phone out of her pocket. She touched the screen. She shook it. She pushed the power button.

"It must have gotten wet," she said.

"You told us not to bring our phones," Claire said.

"Because I wanted you to experience the great outdoors."

"Well, the great outdoors ain't so great right now," Claire shot back.

"We can do better," Honey said. "Maybe even

keep the rain off us. Let's put up a tent."

"They're all wet." Becky peered through the dark to see her tent crumpled behind a tree.

"But they'll keep the water off us." Honey switched on her hat light that she'd recovered and pulled her tent out of the pile. The poles were still in it, making it heavy and awkward. She looked above her. The Mummy Mates flag drooped from the branch. That would work as well as a shelter, if they could tie the bottom of it up so it was flat over their heads.

And the one way to get Claire to stay on the team was to let her think she was the captain.

"Claire," Honey said. "Can you figure out a way to tie the flag up over our heads?"

Claire looked up and blinked as the rain poured onto her face. "You can't do that? It's not hard."

Honey chomped down on her tongue

to keep from telling Claire she didn't need her help. After they turned the flag into a shelter, they huddled beneath the small rectangle, shivering with teeth clattering. Every once in a while Honey would take a deep breath and tell herself that she was going to force her skin to stop puckering and she would feel warmer, but the next gust of wind would blow and the goosebumps would pop out all over again. To help pass the time, Trout led them in choruses of *Bingo* and *Row, Row, Row Your Boat*—which Honey thought was more than appropriate under the circumstance.

The sky began to lighten about the time the rain let up. Honey's stomach growled, but she didn't think she could stomach another peanut butter-macaroni and cheese. Hopefully someone had a plan.

"Breakfast food?" Brianna said. "No problem." She pulled two bananas and a jar of Nutella out of her soggy backpack. Honey's stomach growled again. When they'd had the planning meeting a month ago, Donna told their parents that they'd be eating warm oatmeal and sausage and gravy for breakfast.

"I call the tortillas," Becky said. She wrung out a pair of socks and hung them on the tree branch to dry. "Tortillas with Nutella will taste just like French crepes."

Leave it to Becky to concoct something fantastic out of the randomness that was Brianna.

83

Honey dumped her backpack out. At least her windbreaker was dry. It'd been on top of her backpack. Everything else ranged from damp to soaked. She grabbed for her windbreaker and felt the pockets. Where was her map? Had it survived?

"Well, do I look different today?" Claire held her arms out to her side and spun slowly.

Besides being dirty and wet, Honey didn't see anything remarkable. Just like every other warm day of the year, Claire had on a sports jersey and gym shorts. On cold days she wore wind pants or ratty jeans. Her baseball cap still had her lamp attached to it, and her blond hair was in braids. Honey looked closer. Ah-ha. Right there.

"I know," Honey said. "You have a zit on your chin."

Claire glared at her. "Do not."

"Yes, you do." Honey poked her finger at the red spot. "You didn't have that yesterday when we got here."

"Maybe it's a bug bite?" Brianna said. "Do you want some of my all-natural bug spray?"

"No." Claire pushed Honey's hand away, then rubbed at her chin. "That's not what I'm talking about."

"Your clothes are wet?" Becky asked. "Usually your clothes are dry, so that's different."

"I can't believe you," Claire said. "Worst friends ever!"

Honey stopped her search for the map and looked up at Claire. "What did we do to you?" Honey asked.

"Today is my birthday." Claire threw her backpack to the ground where it splashed in a puddle. "And no one said anything about it."

Honey looked at Becky who scrunched up her face and shrugged. "Why didn't you tell us?" Honey asked.

"Because you're my friends. You should've known."

"We're sorry," Becky said. "I feel awful."

"I don't," Honey said. "Am I supposed to have everyone's birthday memorized? If you want us to celebrate your birthday, you should've invited us to a party or something."

"You are so mean," Claire said. "See if I tell you Happy Birthday when it's your birthday."

Honey was tired, wet and hungry. She

didn't have the energy to fake sympathy. "When is my birthday? Do you even know?"

Claire shoved her face closer to Honey's. "It's not the same day as mine. I know that!"

"That's my point. You want us to feel sorry for you, but you don't know our birthdays."

"Girls!" Trout yelled, then quoted, "A Spooky Scout doesn't look for differences but for common ground in all mankind..."

"I see common ground," Honey said. "None of us know when the others' birthday is, only Claire has decided to be a baby about it."

"I'm not a baby," Claire said.

"Then stop whining and get ready to go. We have another full day of hiking if we're going to reach the next campground before night."

"I don't have any shoes! They washed away last night and I've been barefoot ever since!" Claire was good and angry now, but at least she wasn't feeling sorry for herself. Honey wouldn't be surprised if she took off running the trail and beat them to the finish. Getting Claire mad was the best way to bring out her competitiveness.

"I have an extra pair of shoes," Brianna said.

"Of course you do," said Claire.

Brianna rummaged in her backpack and pulled out a pair of house slippers. They were tall booties covered in hot pink faux fur with a criss-cross pattern in sequins on them. They looked really cozy for around the house. Marching over a mountain, not so much.

87

Claire rolled her eyes, but took them anyway. "Thanks."

"Oh, my backpack weighs a ton." Trout had managed to get hers right-side up this time. "Everything is wet."

"We can't wait for it to dry," Honey said. "It'd take hours."

"Especially the sleeping bags," Brianna said. "It's like carrying an extra gallon of milk in my bag."

Did Brianna have a gallon of milk in her bag? Honey wouldn't be surprised.

"We'll just have to go slower," Trout said. "Let your stuff dry while we eat and anytime we stop. Hopefully by tonight we'll be good as new."

88

"Without shoes? Without food?" Claire peeled a banana and shoved it into her mouth.

"But we'll be that much closer to earning our patches," Honey said.

They all sat around as Becky spread Nutella on the tortillas. Brianna sliced up the other banana to share with everyone.

"I'm just surprised at how fast the tents washed away," Becky said. "I thought the stakes were supposed to hold them."

Honey remembered what her father had

told her about the stakes. She only wished that she had remembered it last night when she'd picked the campsite. "My father said the stakes have to be set in a firm foundation. If they are only in something soft like sand,

they won't stand up against any trouble. At the first push, they'll give up and you'll lose everything."

"But it's so much harder to get the stakes in the ground," Becky said.

Honey didn't say it aloud, but she could hear her father's voice, "Strong foundations take time, but once they're there, they'll hold against the fiercest storms. Build your tent on something soft and easy, and you'll have nothing supporting you when trouble comes."

Brianna was quietly singing as she fixed more breakfast,

"The wise man built his house upon a rock,
The wise man built his house upon a rock."

Honey knew the song. Sometimes stories like that seemed like fairy tales, but what had happened last night was real life. She'd be more careful where she built her tent tonight. She didn't like the feeling of having everything falling down around her head. Being trapped by your own poor planning wasn't a mistake Honey wanted to repeat.

And neither was this hiking trip. They had to reach the bottom of the mountain by Sunday at noon or it was all for nothing.

OUTNUMBERED

Whenever Honey saw the word "Laundry" on her chore chart at home, she shuddered. The part she hated the most was pulling the wet clothes out of the washer and putting them into the dryer. She didn't like how the cold, damp clothes made her fingers feel, plus the clothes weighed a ton.

Now she had a whole bag of wet clothes on her back. The straps of her turtle backpack dug into her shoulders and sometimes drips of cold water fell out of the bottom of the turtle and landed on the backs of her ankles.

"Honey's turtle is peeing on her," Claire said.

"Shut up, Claire." Honey said.

"Girls, girls," Trout said. "Put sunshine in your smile and the sky will never be cloudy."

If Trout really believed that, why didn't she smile away that thunderstorm last night? They could've used some sunshine.

Becky plowed on ahead of them, but then stopped where the trail branched. She bent down and lifted a board out of the mud.

"Look at this." She held it out to them. It said Perdition Pass.

"Great," Trout said. "Then we go that way."

Honey shook her head as she studied the muddy puddle it'd been soaking in. "Which way? Which trail was on the sign pointing to?"

"The trails are identical. Like twin trails," Claire said.

"Except one leads to the finish line, food, dry clothes, our parents and a hiking patch," Becky said.

93

"Yeah," Claire said. She picked up a rock and tossed it down the left trail. "And one leads to bears, hypothermia, and certain death."

Honey grabbed the sign and held it up. "Look. It has an arrow. We just have to follow—" but then something terrible happened. The arrow spun in the opposite direction. "Drat!" she said. "It spins. The arrow spins. Now we can't be sure which way to go."

Trout just kind of stood there, tapping her walking stick on the ground.

Obviously, Trout didn't have a clue. With a sigh, Honey dropped her backpack and found her map. She unfolded it on the ground.

"Here are the trails," she said tapping the map like Trout's stick.

"But which way are we headed now?" Becky asked.

94

Proud of any excuse to use her compass, and thrilled that she had listened to Dad when he explained how to use it when you're lost, Honey opened it up. She adjusted her hat to a more professional angle, then held the compass flat in her hand.

"The arrow is pointing to me, so behind us is north."

Trout looked at the compass. "Okay, so if we're facing south, which trail do we take?"

Honey spun her map around. She looked up at the two trails, then down again. She had to be sure. She was responsible for the group and she did not want a repeat of the campsite fiasco. "We go left," she said.

"Left it is," Trout said. She pointed her walking stick toward the right trail.

"Your other left," Claire said.

"Let's get a picture," Becky said. She took the camera off her neck, then turned as they gathered at the crossroads. "Where's Brianna?"

95

"I'm coming." Brianna trudged up the hill under her gigantic backpack. "I didn't get lost. I promised my mom I wouldn't get lost, and so far I've found you all every time." She slid the backpack off her shoulders. It fell with a noise that sounded like jingle bells and breaking glass.

"What all is in there?" Honey asked.

Brianna swung her arms over her head

and rolled her shoulders. "Just stuff I thought we'd need. But it's getting so heavy. I might have to leave some of it behind."

"Ya think?" Claire rolled her eyes. "You should've known you couldn't carry that all the way and keep up. You aren't any kind of athlete."

Becky stepped between them. "She's trying her hardest. Besides, we're awfully glad she brought the macaroni and tortillas, aren't we?"

Honey took a deep breath and blew it out her nose. If only Brianna had brought something more substantial. She slipped the compass into her pocket. She bent her head back and allowed the warming rays of sun breaking through the forest canopy to bathe her face. "It's getting warmer," she said.

"If we walk faster, we'll have longer to lay our stuff out before it gets dark," Honey said. "Our sleeping bags will be drier."

"I can walk faster," Claire said. "Anything to reach the end and get off this mountain." She looked at the slippers on her feet. "You know, these shoes haven't been that bad actually. I wouldn't want to kick a soccer ball in them, but for walking around all day, they've done just fine."

"My sneakers are about dry." Becky looked down at her feet. She wrinkled her nose. "What's that on my socks? Maybe I'm just hungry, but it looks like someone has dusted me with cinnamon."

Brianna bent closer. "I don't think cinnamon can crawl."

Becky's laugh was more than a little nervous. "I'm sure it's just dirt, Brianna. I didn't really think it was cinnamon."

"But it really is crawling. Look!"

Honey stepped closer and watched as the dark speckles of dirt seemed to wiggle. Becky's legs did look like they'd been dusted, but the dust was slowly moving upward, traveling from where her sock ended up to her knee.

"Arghhhh...." Becky jumped and began a frantic dance. "Get them off of me! Get them off!"

Was this the Becky, who could catch mice and wasn't afraid of bats and snakes? Honey was more than a little surprised that Becky was afraid of moving pieces of dirt.

"Calm down," Claire said. "They're so tiny,

they can't hurt you."

"Yes, they can," Brianna said as she took the camera out of Becky's hand. "She might as well freak out. Those are seed ticks and they're probably biting her in a thousand different places right now. She should be panicking. Just think off all the blood they're drinking."

And that was all it took to drive Becky over the edge. Swiping at her legs, she ran in circles and tried to stomp off the ticks.

"What are seed ticks?" Honey asked.

Trout shook her head just like people do when they are looking down at a casket. "Seed ticks are really baby ticks. Thousands of them can live together. Becky must've stood in their nest."

"Looks like that natural stuff didn't work?" Honey asked.

"I have DEET!" Claire screamed. She ripped through her backpack until she found a spray can. Then she began chasing Becky around spraying it at her.

"That's insect repellent," Honey said. "Too late for that. It won't kill them."

"But it'll make them hate themselves. They'll probably want to take a bath which means, they'll no longer be sucking on Becky's blood," Claire said.

100 "I'm going to be sick," Becky cried.

Honey looked down where they were standing. Could this be the nest? "Everyone, pick up your backpacks. Let's not stand here anymore."

Trout grabbed Becky's backpack and led Becky to a less grassy area. Becky sat on the ground and pulled off her shoes and socks. Now that Honey knew what those specks were, she shuddered to see them crawling around on Becky's white socks. Even worse, there was a solid dark ring on Becky's ankles where the socks ended. A whole nation of seed ticks dined at the Becky Young buffet.

Claire, over-zealous as ever, was dousing herself until rivers of bug spray ran down her legs, while Becky and Brianna were trying to scrub the ticks off her skin. Trout was helping, but every once in a while she looked at the black beneath her fingernails and grimaced.

Honey had an idea. "First aid kit?" she said.

"I did bring that," Trout said, forgetting that if Honey hadn't reminded her it would be sitting next to the cooler with their food.

Honey opened it, then grabbed the roll of medical tape. She pulled off a strip and she stuck it to Becky's shin.

"I don't like this idea," Becky groaned.

"I think we're out of options," Honey said. Then with a flourish, she ripped the tape off.

"Owww...." Becky grabbed at her skin. "That hurt! I don't shave my legs, remember?"

Honey flipped the tape over. Along with

Becky's leg hair was several dozen squirming ticks stuck in the goop.

"Look!" Honey held it up for Becky to see.

Becky drew back to get some distance. "I don't want them on my face."

"But they're trapped. It's a tick trap. Isn't that cool?" Why weren't they as impressed with her ingenuity?

"It hurt, but do it again," Becky said. "Just

get them off of me."

Honey ripped off strips for Brianna and Trout and soon they were all peeling off ticks and the top layer of Becky's epidermis.

Becky flopped on her back and covered her eyes. "I thought I loved all animals. Especially baby animals. How could they do this to me?"

"Your blood tastes just as good as anybody's," Honey said.

"Hey, guys," Claire called. "Look this way!"

Honey turned with a piece of tick-covered tape and saw Claire holding Becky's camera. There was a sudden flash. Claire smiled. "If that isn't a winning friendship picture, I don't know what is."

Friendship? Claire had a point. If friendship meant helping someone out when they were in serious, disgusting trouble, then this moment was a friendship moment indeed.

104

LIGHTENING THE LOAD

The ticks had finally all been trapped in the sticky purgatory of medical tape and disposed of. There were no trash cans around and Trout didn't believe in littering, so an impromptu cremation service was held. Even tender-hearted Becky wasn't sad to see the little blood-suckers go up in smoke. Especially since she was covered in bite marks.

All that work, all that time, and they were still at the crossroads, but at least they knew which way to go. Thanks to Honey and her compass, they made the correct turn and took off with speed, hoping to make up for the de-ticking delay.

Everyone was keeping up the pace— everyone except for Brianna.

"Where is she?" Claire propped her foot up on a fallen log. "She's so slow."

"I'm coming," Brianna said. "I'm not lost. I can hear you all the time."

"Maybe we should slow down," Becky said. "She is carrying a lot."

"That's her own fault," Claire said. "No one forced her to pack all that stuff."

The rustling behind them got louder. The branches opened and Brianna walked up to them.

"Sorry, I'm walking as fast as I can, Honey. That last hill was really steep." Then she got distracted. She pulled acorns out of her pocket, and knelt. She rolled the acorn beneath the tree branches. "Here, squirrel. I brought you a snack."

"She's even carrying food for the squirrels." Claire said. "No wonder she can't keep up."

Trout tapped Brianna on the shoulder. "Brianna, dear, you have to keep up with us. Remember what you promised your mother? We don't want you to get lost again. No more Mayflower incidents, OK?"

"I'm not going to get lost. I'm keeping up."

Trout turned to the other girls. "There you go. She's going to keep up. Now, let's get moving. The sun is overhead and I'm hungry."

They took off again, but the mountain grew incredibly steep. The muscles in Honey's legs began to burn. She got a stitch in her side. Next to her, Becky was wheezing. Even Trout was having trouble keeping up with Claire. They continued on for what felt like miles. With each step Honey thought she could go no further, but then she pushed herself just a little more. Step after step they were making progress. She didn't want to be the one to give up first, even though her ankle still hurt a little.

But where was Brianna?

Honey had just decided to wait on her again, when the trail broke open to a little campground. There was a fire-pit already put together and two outhouses. And what do you know? There was Brianna. She'd kept up, but her backpack had not.

"Where's your stuff?" Honey asked.

"I had to keep up, so I left it behind."

"You what?" Honey's mouth dropped open.

"I took it off. Claire was right, I can't walk fast enough carrying all that stuff. I'll just do without."

Trout's eyes bugged. "You need a sleeping bag and tent," she said.

"I've got my jacket. It's just for one more night."

"Not like our tents and sleeping bags kept us warm last night," Honey added. In a way, she envied Brianna. When something stopped making sense, she stopped doing it. Honey sometimes wished she was brave enough to leave behind the stuff that slowed her down on her journey.

"You can sleep in my tent if you want," Becky said. "We would have helped you carry your stuff. You just had to ask."

Claire rolled her eyes. No, Honey wouldn't ask Claire to help carry Brianna's stuff. That was for certain.

"C'mon girls," Trout said. "Let's get our wet stuff out so it can be drying while we eat and rest."

The grassy clearing was catching plenty of sun at that moment. Honey unzipped her sleeping bag so it'd lay out flat. Ditto the tent, although she'd need to flip them over soon. Out came pjs, socks, T-shirts and shorts. The rain had drenched everything, so it all needed air. Soon the area looked like the time her dog, Half Moon, had dragged the laundry basket out the door and all over the backyard.

Claire clapped her hands together when she was finished. "What's for lunch?" she asked.

Trout turned to look at Brianna. "Any tortillas and ketchup left?"

Brianna shrugged. "They're in my backpack."

"I don't want to eat that anyway." Claire unzipped her bag. "I guess it's time to break out the trail mix."

Honey did the same. She turned the sack of dry, dusty trail mix slowly and watched the peanuts and raisins tumble over each other. Trail mix sounded like fun for a snack, but when you were starving, it was like eating the erasers off of pencils. She sloshed her canteen around. It sounded like it was half-full of warm water. She tried not to think about what her parents and brothers were doing at that moment. Probably eating at one of those restaurants that put chocolate chips, whip cream, and gummy bears on your pancakes. She looked again at the trail mix. She could do this.

"Hey!" Claire's voice rang out over the clearing. "What are you eating?"

Honey followed her pointing finger to where Brianna sat with a ham sandwich, a bag of chips and a pudding cup. Brianna lowered the cold soda she was drinking and looked down.

"What? This? This is my lunch."

Honey's mouth watered. "Where in the

111

world did you get that?" she asked.

"I brought an insulated freezer bag with sandwiches for everyone. Mom thought of the pudding cups. And of course, drinking water gets old. I thought it'd be nice to have some variety."

Claire looked at Honey. Honey looked at Claire. "Do you mean that your backpack has sandwiches for all of us?"

Brianna nodded. "And chips. And pudding. And sodas, although I couldn't find a cream soda for Becky, so I had to bring her second favorite, lemon-lime."

"You have lemon-lime?" Becky licked her lips. "I lost a lot of blood. I need lemon-lime. Where is that backpack?"

Honey could've sworn that nothing in the world could've made her go back down the trail, but hunger made you do funny things. And that's how Claire and Honey found themselves lugging Brianna's too heavy backpack up the mountain to the clearing. Each of them held one of the straps and they dragged it on the ground between them.

"Smile!" Becky said, and snapped a picture.

"You don't know how much self-control it took to bring it here before we ate," Claire said.

"Self-control?" Honey said. "I stopped you. It had nothing to do with self-control."

Brianna hurried to meet them and dug out the insulated bag. "I thought Trout would have dinner for us the first night, so I was saving this for lunch. I really wanted to bring enough for everyone, but it was just too heavy. That's why I had to put my lunch in my pocket."

Honey dropped to the ground. If she'd been tired before, now she was exhausted. But it was nothing that a sandwich, deep fried potato chips, chocolate pudding and a soda couldn't fix.

They ate in silence, too tired to talk. Only

Brianna walked around trying to find a squirrel to feed.

After Honey had drained the can of every last drop, she fell on her back. The night before had been disastrous. Only a few hours of sleep before the rain started falling and her tent decided to smother her. Now the sun was out. It warmed her skin while drying her clothes. If she could rest for just a few minutes...

"Rise and shine, Spooky Scouts! It's time to march!"

Honey groaned and rolled to her side. Sleep hazed her thoughts and clouded her eyes. Where was she? What time was it? Claire sat up, her ponytail crooked and full of grass. She'd taken off her pink slippers to sleep. She wiggled her toes in the cool grass. Brianna was still exploring the area around the camp, looking for more treasure to put in her pockets. Becky snored softly as Trout stood over her.

"C'mon, Becky. Time to hit the trail."

"She's like that all the time," Honey said. "Waking her up is nearly impossible."

Honey watched sleepy Claire try to pull on her shoes. She managed to get them on the wrong feet but didn't seem to notice. Brianna skipped to where Honey was sitting. She pulled a short white and black feather from her braid.

Honey wrinkled her nose. "Did you find those feathers? You shouldn't put them in your hair, Brianna. They could have mites."

Brianna shrugged. Then she held the feather like a pencil and she drew a path on Becky's tick-feasted legs.

The bites glared an angry red and some of them filled up like tiny little clear bubbles. Becky groggily brushed her hand across her shin. She frowned, then scratched at the spot.

"Ouch!" she cried and she sat bolt upright. "I've got to keep scratching, but it hurts."

Honey had had insect bites before where you wanted to scratch off your skin, but the pain was too bad. She should sympathize, but instead she was studying the bites and wondering what sort of picture she could create doing dot-to-dot on Becky's legs.

"I can't stop scratching," Becky said.

"I'll get you some of my bug spray," said Claire.

"No," Trout said. "That will burn like crazy. She needs some cream."

"I couldn't find cream soda," Brianna pouted. "Just lemon-lime."

"Lemon-lime will sting too," said Claire.

"You are not pouring soda on my bug bites," Becky cried.

Honey had to agree with Becky. It'd be sticky, and just think of the ants she'd attract. That was the last thing she needed.

"Let me look in the first aid kit," Trout said. The lures on her hat jingled as she jogged to retrieve it. Soon she returned with a tube of cream. "Whoever packed this probably had no idea someone could have so many bites. It might only work one time."

Becky held out her hand for Trout to squirt the cream into it. Then she slathered the cream all over her legs.

"Ahhhh...."

117

"Okay, girls. Let's repack, then get going.

We have a lot of ground to cover before we set up camp tonight."

Honey rolled her sleeping bag up. She had to admit, it was drier and probably lighter. Everyone else was exclaiming over the same thing. Everyone except Brianna. She was luring a squirrel closer and closer.

The squirrel watched her with shiny black eyes. Brianna didn't move a muscle, just kept the acorn in her outstretched fingers. With quick, jerky movements, the squirrel grabbed the acorn and raced away from her.

Brianna's eyes lit up. "Did you see that?" She took the ends of her braids and swung them around as she did a little dance in the clearing.

RECALCULATING

"Has everyone used the outhouse?" Trout asked.

"Yeah," Claire said. But she whispered to

Honey, "I'm surprised Trout doesn't take her poop book in there to see what she can identify."

The bags were nearly packed. Honey looked at Brianna's heavy backpack. "Brianna, are you going to carry that now?"

Everyone stopped what they were doing and turned around to look. Brianna chewed on the end of her braid. "It's really heavy."

"Do you have more food in there?" Claire asked.

"Sure."

"Like what?"

"Oh, I can't remember everything. I know I have more drinks and snacks. My grandma made cookies..."

"We have to take that bag," Honey said. "Maybe we should draw straws to see who carries it."

"No one can carry two bags," Becky said. "Besides, Brianna could carry something."

True. Brianna could handle a normal sized bag. Honey looked at her options. "Here's what we're going to do. We'll take turns carrying her bag and she'll carry ours. That way no one is stuck with the heavy bag for long."

"Not it!" Claire said.

"Really, Claire?" Honey said.

"It's my birthday."

"I'll go first," Honey said. Because a leader wasn't afraid to do the hard work as an example to her followers. She handed Brianna her turtle backpack.

Brianna turned it around and stared the turtle. She stared straight into his googlie eyes. "I won't be catching any squirrels wearing this. It'll scare them away."

"You shouldn't be catching squirrels anyway," Honey said. "They bite."

"They've never bitten me," Brianna said.

"Have you ever caught one?"

"I've fed one, but not really caught it."

Honey raised an eyebrow. "Which path do we take now?"

Honey pulled out the map and compass. She flipped the map and consulted the compass, which pointed at her again.

"Yep," she said. "This path behind me."

She shouldered Brianna's backpack, which was terribly heavy, no fooling, even with five less sodas and pudding cups.

"I don't want to question you," Becky said. Becky had played too many games against Honey to challenge her carelessly. "But isn't that the trail we came in on?"

Claire put her hand on her hip. "It is, but that can't be right. We'd be backtracking."

"Are you sure about that map?" Trout asked.

"Yes," Honey said. She held it flat while the girls and Trout gathered around. "This way is north on the paper, and my compass says that..." Her compass wasn't pointing the same way anymore. It wasn't pointing at the trail. It was still pointing at her, but she wasn't facing the same direction.

123

"There's something wrong," she said.

"Yeah, like you can't read a map," Claire huffed.

But Honey was on the scent of a mystery. Slowly she turned. The compass was broken, because no matter how she turned, it always pointed at her.

"Let me try it," Claire said.

Honey passed the compass to her and as soon as it left Honey's hand, the needle swung to point toward Claire.

Claire repeated Honey's move of turning a circle. "It's broken. It's not moving," she said.

"Let me see." Brianna bent her head over the compass and the needle immediately swung to her. She eased out of the circle, and the compass clicked along toward Claire.

The answer to the compass mystery was on the tip of Honey's tongue. Something was interfering with the needle. Something that would throw its reading off...

Her gaze traveled up to the hats the girls wore. The answer struck her. The lights on their hats. They were held in place by magnets. Honey's stomach wobbled. She was wearing a magnet while trying to use a compass. Didn't she know better than that?

"It's the hats," she said. "The magnets are making the compass point to us." How long had this been going on? She felt like crying. They could have been going the wrong direction ever since the fork in the trail that morning. So much for always being right. Honey scuffed her shoes in the dirt. Her mistake had cost the whole group.

"Oh, Honey." Becky blinked back tears. "You mean we came all this way, but we've been going in the wrong direction?"

"Un-be-lievable!" Claire swung her hands into the sky. "We've wasted all this time? We're never going to make it to the end of the trail by noon tomorrow. It's physically impossible."

Honey could understand why Claire was so upset. She was that mad and more, but she felt worse because of all they'd been through. If she hadn't made that mistake, Brianna wouldn't have had to carry her bag all the extra way, Becky wouldn't have stood in the tick nest, and Claire...well, Claire wouldn't be happy either way.

Trout came and put her arm around

Honey's shoulder. "Don't take it too hard, Honey. We all make mistakes."

Honey's shoulders drooped. Trout was trying to be nice, but now Honey was worried. Maybe Trout had been a spelling bee champion and award-winning essay writer at one time. Then one day, she got everyone lost, and from then on her future was ruined. After that mistake, she had to wear floppy hats with fishing lures for the rest of her life. Was that what happened? Was Honey destined to be a Trout?

Now they knew that the compass was going the right way, they had to backtrack down the trail to the turn-off, the very place they'd been that morning, a fact that the girls couldn't forgive.

"We're never getting home," Becky said.

"Just think, we walked all the way up that hill for nothing," Claire said. "And now we have to climb it again on another side."

"But we had a good time," Brianna said.

"Our clothes are mostly dry and we had a good lunch and we even had outhouses!"

"That's right, Brianna," Trout said. "Look on the bright side." Then she started singing,

"We come from Sleepy Hollow, shout it out.
We are the best, there is no doubt.
It's not that we mean to flaunt, but everyone wants to be a Spooky Scout!"

Honey walked fast to pass the other girls. For one thing, she didn't want to hear Claire's never-ending complaints. Secondly, Brianna's backpack was so heavy she figured she needed to be ahead so when she started slowing down, she'd have some breathing room. And she even had to put up with the Sleepy Hollow song with the one word that doesn't rhyme. But she figured she was the only one who cared about such things. Honey believed in the integrity of iambic pentameter while others did not.

At the next wide place in the trail, Honey passed Becky and caught up with Trout.

127

Here was her chance to see what had changed their guide from a normal person into Trout—the goofy, fishing lure wearing woman who'd never completed a hike on her own.

And because Honey couldn't think of a way to ask how someone turned out to be such a nerd, she asked about her name. "So why do they call you Trout?"

"It comes from when I was in the Jack-o -Lantern level. I was earning my Team Spirit patch."

"Oh yeah, the one where you have to make a piece of art to celebrate the Spooky Scouts?"

"That's the one. I had a little bit of a speech problem, and had to go see the speech therapist every week at school. Turns out I didn't always process sounds right. I could hear, but for some reason I didn't hear like everyone else. Anyway, I worked on my project for weeks. I took a silver sleeping bag and cut arm holes. I painted it up really cute. It looked wonderful. I'd never worked so hard in my life for something.

Then the rally came and I was so excited. I knew everyone would be impressed."

Trout pushed a log out of the path. Black, hard-shelled bugs scattered when she picked it up and heaved it to the side.

"The time for the performance came and I was so nervous. All the Spooky Scouts were there, even the Tombstone Teens. The other Jack-o-Lantern's presented their Team Spirit pictures or songs. Someone even designed a T-shirt, but nothing as elaborate as my project. When it was time to take the stage, I waddled out wearing my painted silver sleeping bag. The fins were carefully pinned on and glittered in the spot light. The giant eyeballs even moved, and fixing that was not easy, let me tell you. I marched up to the microphone and I sang,

"We come from Sleepy Hollow, shout it out.
We are the best, there is no doubt.
It's not that we mean to flaunt, but everyone wants to be a SPOTTED TROUT!"

Honey stopped in her tracks. Her mouth dropped open. "A spotted trout? You thought the club name was Spotted Trouts?"

"Well, I was young and didn't read much yet. And we did have that one handbook with the fish on it..."

"Oh yeah," Honey remembered the Jack-o-Lantern's outdoor handbook. "What happened?"

130   Trout shrugged. "Everyone nearly fell out of their chairs laughing. My scout friends were laughing so hard it made my chest hurt. I looked at the Scout Master to see if she was going to help me, but she was doubled over, too. It was the most horrible feeling."

"That's awful. I wouldn't ever come back to a group that treated me like that." Honey felt bad. How many times had she doubted Trout, or poked fun at her? Trout always did her best.

"It hurt my feelings, but then I started thinking about it. You know, I was proud of the job I did on that costume." Trout picked up a small, flat stone and tossed it into the woods. "It did look like a trout. A big, silvery trout."

Honey smiled. Trout smiled. Then they both laughed.

"It was kind of funny now that some time has gone by. Life is like that."

"Yeah, I know what you mean." Honey had remembered the terrible paint disaster right before the Valentine's dance. It was pretty tragic at the time. But now she could laugh about it—a little anyway.

131

"So maybe I made a mistake," Trout said. "But everything else I did was right."

"That's right," Honey said. "You still did an awesome job."

"Just like you," Trout said. "Maybe you made a mistake with the compass, but the fact that you brought a compass, brought a map, and you weren't afraid to be a leader, that means more than the one little mistake.

It's easy for people to say you did something wrong when they aren't accomplishing anything. At least you're trying."

Honey didn't like it that she was the reason the troop was lost. It made her want to stop helping and never offer her advice or help again. But wasn't it better to offer help and suggestions than to not say anything? After all, there was still a pretty good chance they would still be lost.

Honey pulled the compass out of her pocket. "And I did solve the problem."

"You sure did," Trout said. "And now you can help us get to that finish line." Trout punched her fist in the air.

She smiled up at Trout. "I'm glad Donna didn't come this time," Honey said. "You're doing a pretty good job all by yourself."

Trout wrapped an arm around Honey's shoulder. "Thanks, Honey Moon. But I'm not in this alone. I've got the help of all you little

Spotted Trouts."

Honey grinned. "To the finish line?"

"To the finish line and those awesome patches," Trout said.

134

BURNING AMBITION

I t was nearly nightfall when they reached the other side of the mountain. Everyone had taken turns helping with Brianna's giant bag during the day. After Honey had carried it awhile, she felt bad for being impatient with

Brianna. She had tried her best to keep up with them, when all along she was carrying twice the load they were. No wonder she kept falling behind. People said you should walk a mile in someone's shoes to understand them. Honey thought carrying their backpack was just as good of a test.

"We are definitely on the right track now." Trout leaned on her walking stick and rubbed her back. "I remember this campground from two years ago."

"Are we going to reach the bottom of the mountain?" Becky took off her hat and fanned herself with it.

Trout lowered her head. "I'm not sure about that." Then she smiled, lifted her eyebrows and in a voice that would only fool pre-schoolers added, "But you guys did a super-fantastic job. Everyone will be so proud of how hard you worked."

Claire was already setting up her tent. "I thought this was gonna be the worst birthday ever. But now I think it's the best."

"The best?" Becky said. "How so?"

"Don't you get it? A flash flood, using the woods for a bathroom, getting lost. My birthday turned into an adventure."

"Yeah," Becky said. "You're right."

"I cannot wait to see what happens next," Claire said.

137

"Next," Becky said. "I hope it's smooth sailing from here on out."

Honey, who had been fussing with her tent chimed in. "What happens next? I hope nothing else happens."

"Awww, c'mon," Claire said. "Where's your team spirit?"

"That's the spirit Claire," Brianna said. She held the tent pole up for Claire. Claire grabbed a rock and hammered the spike into the ground. "And the good news is that you're still one year older."

The troop got their tents set up in a neat semi-circle.

"Ok," Claire said. "What are we going to eat?"

"I don't have any food left," Brianna said.

Honey's ears perked up. "What? You said you had cookies." Honey had been thinking about those cookies all day long.

"Oh, I have dessert, just no food."

They all heaved a sigh of relief. Even Trout had looked worried. "I knew camping was good exercise, but I didn't expect to be put on a starvation diet."

"No diet," Brianna said. "That's for sure. We'll have s'mores."

S'mores?!! Maybe the girls were giddy from lack of sleep and intense hunger but Honey felt like crying from happiness. They jumped up and down cheering. Brianna had saved the day. Honey thought the hike was a total disaster, but Brianna had managed to give them the thing they wanted most in the world at that moment.

"S'mores?" Claire said. "In that case I guess I'll stay awake."

"Quick," Becky gasped. "Let's take a friendship picture."

The girls gathered together. Trout said, "Let me take it so you can all be in it."

"No," Becky said. "We'll do a selfie. Come on and get in with us."

Trout tossed her walking stick aside, removed her hat and fluffed up her short hair. Taking the camera and holding it out at arms' length, she instructed them to press their faces close together.

"Cheese," she said.

Then snap. It was a friend picture for the entire group.

Before the flash had stopped turning her eyes colors, Honey had started organizing the troops.

"Brianna you get the supplies ready. Claire you help Trout build the fire. Becky, find sticks for the marshmallows."

Everyone sprang to action. Becky whispered something about singing Happy Birthday to Claire, which was a great idea. They were so excited, but Honey couldn't celebrate outright. Not now, anyway. Not when they'd failed.

The sun was down by the time all the tents were set up. Brianna kept rummaging in the trees for things, always on a treasure hunt of her own, but she'd kept her promise. So far she had not gotten lost. Trout and Claire talked about the Boston Bruins by the roaring fire, waiting for everyone to finish the chores and start the marshmallows.

Becky came back with five, long sticks and passed them around.

"Hold them in the fire first to burn off any germs," Trout instructed.

The girls obeyed, but as Honey's eyes became fixated on the flames, she realized that she was in danger of falling asleep right there at the campfire. Was she content with failing? Had she run out of ambition?

141

The troop passed the marshmallow bag around. Honey was so hungry, that she toasted hers too quickly. It caught fire. She huffed and puffed the flames out, but she didn't care. She was going to eat the black, sticky mess anyway. Taking two graham crackers and a piece of chocolate, she pulled the goopy lump off the stick. Who cared if she ate a little bit of tree bark along with her dinner? When you're hungry enough, you'll eat anything.

"Happy Birthday to you...." It was Brianna singing. She was carrying a plastic container of Grandma's sugar cookies to Claire. Claire's eyes shined in the firelight. "Happy Birthday, Claire."

"How did you do that?" Claire asked. "I didn't think any of you knew."

"Your mom asked my grandma to make them for your birthday. She knew you love Grandma's cookies and it would be too hard for me to carry a cake on the trail."

"I have the best mom." Claire looked around the circle. "I should have known she'd do something like this. And I guess I should have known you guys would do something for my birthday. I have the best friends in the whole entire world."

Claire took a cookie in one hand and her marshmallow roasting stick in the other. Honey really hadn't remembered Claire's birthday, but she was glad Brianna had. And it looked like there was one more surprise to go.

Claire was still roasting her marshmallow when Brianna returned with an insulated freezer bag. The silver foil cover caught the firelight and made it sparkle like magic.

"I have a gift, too," Brianna said.

"From my mom?"

"No, from me."

Honey felt her eyebrows rise. She couldn't figure it out. The bag used to have the sodas and pudding cups in it. It should be empty now. Why did it look so heavy?

143

Claire didn't notice. She licked the icing from the cookies off her fingers and reached for the bag. Keeping her stick in the fire for another toasted s'more, Claire unzipped the freezer bag.

"What's in there? It's too dark to see." She held the bag between her feet.

"Turn on your headlamp," Brianna said.

Claire reached up to switch it on.

Honey was just about to remind Claire that her marshmallow was in the fire, when everything went berserk.

The light from Claire's headlamp shone in the bag, and a furry blur came leaping out, right in her face.

Honey jumped back in terror. They were under attack. Claire screamed bloody murder and shoved the bag away, but it was too late.

The squirrel had gripped her shirt right at the collar and wouldn't let loose.

"Don't hurt it," Brianna cried.

"It's trying to eat my face off," Claire yelled. Both of her eyes were closed, but she stumbled away from the fire, hitting at the creature.

"It's not hurting you." Becky always had a soft spot for animals—unless they were seed ticks.

145

"Get it off of me!!" Brianna and Becky chased Claire who was running around the camp waving a burning marshmallow and trying to see over a terrified squirrel. Honey would act the same way if it happened to her. But it wasn't happening to her, so instead she grabbed Becky's camera and started taking pictures.

"I can't believe you care more about this animal than you care about my safety," Claire said. "And it's my birthday!"

"The squirrel is your birthday present." Brianna was huffing and trying to catch her faster friend. "I spent this whole trip trying to catch one for you."

Trout stood guard over the fire pit to make sure Claire didn't blindly stumble into it. She seemed to be enjoying this as much as Honey was. That is until Claire suddenly turned and bumped right into Becky's tent.

Claire pulled her stick away from the tent, but it was too late. The sticky, burning, marshmallow stuck fast to the side. The flame caught and spread across the nylon material as quickly as the wave of ticks did on Becky.

"My stuff!" Becky yelled. She ducked her head inside the tent, but Honey caught her by the arm and pulled her out.

"You can't go in there. Who cares about your sleeping bag?"

Obviously, the squirrel didn't care, because at the first big flame, he jumped off Claire and scurried into the woods. They all turned and watched it run away.

"Good-bye, little friend," Brianna said. Trout patted her on the back as it disappeared. And when they turned around, they saw an even bigger disaster—the total annihilation of their camp. The fire had spread to the other tents.

Their tents were a smoldering mess. Only Trout's tent was left standing.

147

"Canvas doesn't burn as fast," Trout said.

"Lucky for you," Claire said.

"What are we going to do now?" Honey asked. Trout's tent wasn't big enough for them all to sleep in.

Without saying a word, Trout walked over to her tent and yanked up the stakes. The poles fell to the ground with a clank as she gathered the tent up and threw it into the pile of burning nylon and hot metal.

The girls stood with their mouths hanging open. Had she lost her mind?

"Why in the world did you do that?" Honey asked.

"We Spotted Trouts are all in this together," she said.

They stood there between the two fires— one of them planned and one of them a total surprise—but Honey couldn't say which one was nicer. The troop formed a semi-circle around the small fires.

"We should let it burn down and then douse the embers with dirt," Trout said. "We must not leave any smoldering ashes."

"Smokey the Bear would be proud," Honey said.

It didn't take too long for the fire to burn itself out. Gray smoke drifted into the night sky as the Spooky Scouts dropped handfuls of dirt on the fire spots. Brianna even found a small spring and brought water back in her hat. "We're supposed to stir the ashes," she said. "I read that once in our handbooks."

Trout used her walking stick to stir the ash piles until there wasn't a hint of smoke or hot embers left.

"That's that," Honey said. "Now what?"

"My backpack won't weigh anything now," Brianna said.

149

"No tent, no sleeping bag," Honey said.

"No food left, either," Claire said.

"Where are we going to sleep?" Becky scratched at her legs.

Honey surveyed the campsite. The fire was out but most of their camping gear was either ruined or wet or covered in mud. She looked around at her friends. They all looked so sad. Even Trout held her hat in her hands and seemed defeated. But then Honey felt something gurgle up inside. And it wasn't burnt marshmallow. No, it was courage and determination. The very things the scouts needed to finish the hike.

"We're not going to sleep," she said. "We're going to earn our patches, even if it means hiking all night."

Trout raised her walking stick into the night sky. "Onward we march. Over hill and over dale."

"Who's Dale?" Brianna asked.

"Not that kind of dale," Honey said. "A dale is a grassy area. Like a valley."

"Onward," shouted Claire and Becky.

"To the finish line," Brianna said.

RACE AGINST THE CLOCK

With their headlamps lit, the five determined hikers set out. When they were sitting around the campfire earlier,

Honey felt like she couldn't keep her eyes open for another moment. But after the squirrel attack, and after the tents caught fire, and Trout threw her own gear into the flames, Honey had never felt better or more wide awake.

Her turtle backpack felt empty compared to what she'd started with. Even Brianna's bag was nearly empty now. The house shoes that Claire was wearing looked ridiculous, but Claire marched on like it was the most natural thing in the world.

152

The five Spooky Scouts marched in the dead of night, their headlamps throwing beams through the shadows of the forest, all in a race to get to the finish line before noon, and since they were hiking all night there was a good chance they'd beat the record by hours!

"I feel pretty good," Claire said. "Nothing like a good hike to exercise the leg muscles. And I am of course a whole year older and that automatically makes me stronger."

Becky bumped her on the shoulder. "So

much older, yeah. And more mature."

Brianna laughed. "Did you really think your mom was going to let you come without a birthday treat? We surprised you."

"That squirrel surprised me." Claire rubbed her neck as she laughed. "If I have rabies, I'm biting you first, Brianna."

Brianna did a ballerina spin in the middle of the trail. Her headlamp looked like a lighthouse beam sweeping through the trees.

"This isn't so bad," Trout said. "I think I like night hiking. It's really kind of peaceful."

But then, in an instant, their smiles turned to gasps as a loud, mournful howl exploded into their quiet walk.

Claire jumped a mile straight up. "What was that?"

"It's Sasquatch!" Becky screamed. "Big Foot is in this forest."

They stopped walking. Honey counted headlight beams. But she only counted four.

"Brianna!" Honey screamed. "Where's Brianna?"

"Oh noooo," Claire yelled. "Big Foot got Brianna!"

Becky started to cry. "I knew it. I knew something horrible would happen."

154   Another howl roared through the trees.

"We have to find her," Trout said. "Come on."

"Maybe we should turn off our headlights," Claire said. "So Big Foot can't see us."

They all clicked off their lights and for a few seconds stood in complete blackness. The only light was from the moon and stars.

"It's beautiful," Becky said.

"Turn your lights back on," Honey said. "It's too dark and besides, Sasquatch can still smell our human scent."

The troop clicked on their lights. They huddled together.

"Let's stick close," Trout said. "Nobody goes off on their own."

"Yeah," Claire said. "Big Foot would just love two tasty scout morsels."

"Stop it," Becky said. "I don't want to get eaten by no Big Foot."

155

Honey whispered, "Briannnna, Briannnnna."

But nothing. The forest grew eerily quiet.

Becky sobbed. "Brianna's gone."

Honey grabbed Becky's shoulders. "Stop it! Stop it! Be strong. She's not gone."

"Let's go," Trout said. "She can't be far."

Trout tapped her walking stick on the

ground. "Sasquatch isn't real. Brianna is just off on another squirrel hunt."

Then they heard laughter. Brianna's laugh. Several pinecones fell from a tree. Honey looked up. "There she is."

"How did you get up there?" Trout asked.

Brianna jumped to the ground. "Easy peazy. Just like the squirrels do."

Becky pulled Brianna in for a hug. "I'm so glad Big Foot didn't get you."

"Big Foot," Brianna said. "I don't have big feet."

They all laughed and set off once again toward the finish line.

"But what was that noise?" Claire asked.

"Let's not think about it," Honey said with a shudder. "Too creepy and why did you climb that tree anyway?"

"I told you. I wanted to be a squirrel."

"Okay, okay. I guess we have to give Brianna a special squirrel patch."

Down the mountain they went. Honey thought the miles sped by. It might have been that they picked up their pace after the whole Big Foot thing. But when they reached the Ghost Quiver Falls area Trout suggested that they take a break.

157

"Ok, troops," she said. "Pick a rock and take a load off."

Honey sat on a large boulder. It was difficult to see, but she could hear the water tripping and falling over the rocks. She liked the sound. It was a peaceful, easy music.

"Ghost Quiver," she said. "Good old Spooky Hollow, right."

"But we're so far from home," Becky said. "Probably has nothing to do with Sleepy Hollow." Becky plunked down next to Honey on the big boulder.

"I know," Honey said "But still. It makes me a little home sick."

"Yeah," Claire said. "Me too."

"But it's so bucolic," Trout, who was sitting very close to Brianna, said.

Honey yawned and stretched. "It is so qui—"

But before she could finish her sentence she heard what sounded like a mournful cry come out of the babbling water.

"Did you hear that?" Honey said.

"I . . . I did," shouted Claire, "and I'm not sticking around to find out who it's coming from."

"Me either," Becky said.

And lickety split the girls grabbed their stuff and took off like frightened deer through the trees.

They ran at full tilt for several yards until

they ran out of steam and slowed their pace.

Trout huffed and puffed. "Jeepers creepers, nothing like a ghostly cry to get the heart pumping, huh girls?"

"I say we rest again," Claire said.

"Me too," Honey said.

But this time the girls joined hands and sat in friendship circle.

159

Honey took a deep breath. "This is nice," she said as she looked into the eyes of her friends. Somewhere in the tiredness, the hunger, and the exhaustion, they'd figured out that they were all on the same team. Whatever slowed one of them down, slowed them all. Whatever hurt one of them, hurt them all. That's what being friends meant. Sharing hurts, sharing burdens and sharing birthday parties. "No matter what happens," Honey said. "We're a team."

They rested a few more minutes before

Trout rousted them into action again.

Onward they marched, stopping only occasionally for a potty break. But the further they went, the dimmer their headlights grew. Only Claire's seemed to glow brighter. Honey removed her hat and tapped the light. "It's almost dead."

"Mine too," Becky said.

"And mine," Trout said.

Honey watched as Brianna's headlight blinked into darkness.

"Okay, troops," Trout said. "Single file. Claire you take the lead because your lamp is bright."

The girls assembled themselves with Brianna in the middle so they could keep a close watch on her.

"Now, put your hand on the shoulder of the girl in front of you. We walk elephant style."

Honey laughed. "Elephant style. This is a first."

"What time is it?" Honey asked after walking what she figured was another mile.

"Don't know," Trout said. "But I hope the sun comes up soon."

"Yeah," Brianna said. "The sun always comes up."

Honey's legs burned as she trudged up a minor hill and then down. But she figured another hill was just ahead. She took a deep breath and let it out slowly. And she was correct. "Another hill? How many hills can one hiking trail have?"

"You can do it Honey Moon," Claire shouted. "We all can do it."

With renewed stamina, Honey and the group trudged up the hill and just as they reached the top, the sky lightened as the sun was finally and thankfully on the rise. Honey swiped tears from her eyes as she remembered a line from another Emily Dickinson poem.

I'll tell you how the sun rose.

A ribbon at a time.

The sun continued to rise, bathing the forest in a pink and orange glow as the troop marched on.

"I think we're getting closer," Trout said. "Maybe a mile further. I recognize these from my other hikes."

Honey stopped walking and looked up through the trees. "What if it's further than we think? What if we don't make it? We don't know how fast to go."

"I don't know about you, but I'm not missing my patch because I wimped out on the last mile," Claire said. "We should run."

Trout leaned on her walking stick. "Everyone is really tired, Claire. And we can't leave anyone behind."

163

"I'm going to run," Brianna said. "Run like a squirrel."

"Me too," Becky said. "Only I'd rather run like an antelope."

Honey was so proud of her team she could hardly stand it. "We can all do this, Trout. So can you. This will be your first hike without Donna. Don't you want to win?"

Trout looked at Honey, and her face filled with determination.

"I want to win super-duper bad," she said. "Let's go!"

With a shout they took off. Honey felt like a deer bounding over roots and dodging between trees where the path was narrow. Once Claire lost a house shoe and they all stopped until she could get it back on. Brianna got winded, but her backpack was so light that Trout carried it as well as her own. Honey's side began to hurt too. Sports weren't really her thing, but winning was. If running was what she needed to do to succeed, then she'd be a runner.

At least for today.

The trees thinned. Metal shimmered through the forest. They were almost there. The ground leveled and they raced to the marker at the edge of the parking lot. Claire reached it first, but instead of tagging it, she turned and waved them all forward.

"C'mon, c'mon," she called.

Honey linked arms with Brianna. "Let's get

164

there together."

Claire, Becky, and Trout waited near the marker. But not for long, because Honey and Brianna were right on their heels.

Honey stretched out her hand. "1...2...3!"

Boom! They all hit the end of the trail at the same time—a five-way tie.

"We did it!" shouted Honey. "We made it the whole way."

"I can't believe it!" Becky said. "We really did it. We hiked the Appalachian Trail."

"A part of it anyway," Claire said.

Brianna knelt and kissed the parking lot gravel. "Thank you for being here," she said. "We sure had a fun hike."

"Like no other," Honey said. She reached out her hand and helped Brianna stand. "I'm proud of you, friend."

Brianna smiled. "And I'm proud of you— friend."

"What time is it?" Honey asked as she swiped more tears from her cheeks. "Does anyone know the time?"

There was no one near the ranger station. And the cars parked in the lot were empty.

"We have to sign in," Trout said. "Everyone signs in at the end of a trail." She pointed to a small box nailed to the top of a post. "Over there. The book is in that box."

"Come on," Honey said.

The girls ran to the post.

"Look," Honey said. "We need to write down the time."

Claire dashed over to the ranger station. She smashed her face against the window. "I can see a clock," she called. "It's 6:52."

Honey gave Trout the pen. "You're the leader. You sign first. And sign your real name. You earned it."

Trout's bottom lip quivered. "Thank you." She put pen to paper. "Matilda Louise Crump. 6:52 AM."

Honey signed next.

Then Becky.

Then Claire, and last but certainly not LOST this time, Brianna, who dotted her "I" with a heart. "For friends," she said.

The troop stood, almost like they were stunned, until Claire broke the silence.

"Matilda Crump?" Claire said.

"That's right," Trout said. "Just call me Matilda the Hiker."

"Come on," Honey said. "Let's go sit at that picnic table."

"Good idea," Matilda said. "Donna won't be here for a few hours."

Honey lay her head on the table. Her eyes were heavy with sleep. Her body ached but her heart was glad. She let her eyes close and . . .

"Rise and shine, Sleepy Heads!! Rise and Shine!!!"

Honey jumped off the bench. "What? What happened? Is it Big Foot?"

Her friends laughed.

"Nope. It's just me," Donna said.

"Donna," Honey shouted. "You're here."

"Yeah," she said. "What happened? Did you girls need rescuing again? Did you sleep here all night? Because I'm sorry, if you didn't cross the finish line on your own then you didn't complete the hike according to Spooky Scout rules."

Trout, er, Matilda pulled herself up to her full height. "As leader of this troop I can say that we crossed the finish line on our own, with no help from the outside, at 6:52 AM. This morning. Five hours early!"

The small troop shouted and cheered.

"See for yourself," Honey said. She pointed to the sign-in book.

Donna checked and said, "Well, I can see that you made it, but who is Matilda Louise Crump? You said you weren't rescued."

"I am Matilda Louise Crump," said the former Trout.

"Really? That's your name? Well, okay then, from now on it's Matilda."

Matilda tapped her walking stick on the ground. The ribbons waved. "I'd like to make an announcement," she said. "These four Mummy Mates have just beat the Spooky Scouts record for completing Perdition Pass. They did not have someone pick them up and they did not cheat. They did it through teamwork, determination, and an unplanned fire loss."

"I guess that's one for the record books then." Donna patted Honey on the back. "Congratulations, girls."

The girls all beamed under Donna's praise.

"Let's go home," Donna said. "Everyone in the bus."

"But not me," Honey said. "My parents are picking me up." Honey felt a wave of disappointment wash over her.

"No they're not," Donna said. "Your mom called and said you had permission to ride the bus home."

"Really?" Honey said.

"Yep," Donna said. "Come on. I'm sure you're all starving. I have snacks and water for everyone."

The girls and Matilda filed into the bus. They went straight for the snacks as Donna turned the ignition. "It's a long ride, so sleep if you gotta."

After munching granola bars and fruit and downing water bottles, the girls settled into their seats and grew quiet. Honey sat near the front and leaned her head against the window and let the events of the last two days filter through her brain. It had been a wild and wooly hike for sure. But they did it.

Without the help of Donna, the Scout Master. We did it, she thought. We all did it. She felt especially proud of Matilda.

And then another thought occurred to her.

"I have a question, Donna." Honey tapped Donna on the shoulder.

"What is it, Honey Bee?"

"If that was the fastest time that trail has ever been hiked, then that means that Trout, I mean Matilda, has the fastest time of any Scout Master, right?"

Honey could see Donna's forehead wrinkle in the rearview mirror. "Err..."

"Honey," Matilda, who was sitting in the seat behind Honey said, "It's not a competition."

Donna looked at them in the mirror. "No, it is a competition. Else we wouldn't keep records. Congratulations, Trout. I mean, Matilda. With an achievement like that, I'd say you're more than qualified as an official Scout Master."

"Hooray," the girls cheered.

"We'll make it official at the patch ceremony," Donna said.

Honey smiled wider than she ever did. The hike had been successful—for everyone.

Donna pulled the bus into the school parking lot where everyone's parents were waiting. Even Matilda's brother was there waiting.

173

"We are number one," shouted Honey. "We are number one!"

Then everyone was chanting as they filed off the bus. "We are number one!"

Honey ran to her parents. "We did it. I will get my patch."

Honey's dad scooped her into his arms. "I knew you could do it."

"I didn't get lost," Honey heard Brianna tell her mother.

"I had the best birthday ever," Claire said to her dad.

"And I need one more picture for my friend-ship badge," Becky said. "Donna, will you take a picture of us with Matilda?"

Honey stood with her friends to mark their

174

accomplishment. More than their patch, it was a test of their abilities, and they had passed. She relished the victory, but she couldn't do much more celebrating or she was going to fall over from exhaustion, right there in the school parking lot.

After the picture, she gratefully handed her backpack to her dad for him to put in the back of the mini-van. Harvest clapped his hands when she got in next to him. Harry said something about her stinky clothes and Mom said, "I bet you have a lot of stories to tell us."

But Honey didn't. Not yet. Instead she rested her head against the window and promised herself right then and there that she would never forget the best weekend of her entire life.

HONEY MOON'S
HIKING SURVIVAL GUIDE

Wow! Now that's what I call an adventure. I thought we were goners for sure a couple of times. But no, we made it. We all made it.

Hiking is fun but it can also be dangerous. That's why I want to share with you some Hiking Survival tips.

1. <u>Never go alone</u>. Always bring a friend with you. And always tell someone exactly where you are going and how long you expect to be there.

2. <u>Bring a charged cell phone</u> and one of those pocket chargers.

3. <u>Bring a compass</u>. But make sure you know how to use it.

4. <u>Stay on the trail</u>. Don't wander away. You could get lost really easy in the woods.

5. <u>First Aid kits</u> are essential. And remember, if you get a blister, don't pop it!

6. You might want to bring <u>a rain poncho</u>—just in case.

7. My dad said <u>a whistle is a good</u> thing to have in case you need to be rescued. It's louder than your voice.

8. Remember to <u>use sunscreen</u>. Even though you are in the woods, it's still a good idea.

9. Wear <u>good hiking boots</u> with heavy socks.

10. And always remember, "<u>LEAVE NO TRACE</u>" when you leave a campsite. Take your trash with you!!!

Honey Moon's CAMPFIRE COOKBOOK

178

Camping always makes me hungry. And there is nothing I love better than some good old fashioned campfire cooking. Hotdogs and hamburgers. S'mores and corn on the cob. But here's a few recipes that can help make your campout a little more gourmet.

Camp Meals for 4 Campers

Chicken and Potatoes

8 chicken breast tenders (raw)
4 potatoes (white or sweet) peeled and sliced thin
2 cans regular cut green beans, drained
1 med. sweet onion, sliced thin (optional)
salt & pepper to taste
Heavy duty aluminum foil

Take 4 pieces of foil, big enough to hold the meal and allow for folding and wrapping.

In each piece of foil, place 2 chicken tenders, 1 sliced potato, 1/2 can of green beans, S&P, and some sliced onion, if you want that.

Bring up two sides, fold them down, and then fold in the open sides. Place in the campfire for approx. 30 minutes. Use long tongs to remove from the fire. Check doneness and refold to cook more, if needed. Be careful - they will be hot - and steam will rise when you open the foil. That can burn, so keep it away from your face.

Optional: Add 1 cup of shredded cheddar cheese.

This can also be done with chopped ham instead of chicken.

Sausage and Peppers
2 pounds of Italian sausage (sweet or hot), raw, cut into slices, 1/2 pound per camper
2 med. sweet onions, sliced thin
2 large red or green peppers, sliced thin
4 plum tomatoes, chopped
Salt, pepper, oregano, basil
2 bags of shredded mozzarella cheese, 2 cups each
Crusty bread or four rolls
Heavy duty aluminum foil

Take 4 pieces of foil, big enough to hold the meal and allow for folding and wrapping.

In each piece of foil, place 1/2 pound of sliced sausage, 1/4 of the sliced onion and peppers, and 1 chopped tomato. Sprinkle seasonings over to taste. Top with 1 cup of cheese. Bring up two sides, fold them down, and then fold in the open sides. Place in the campfire for approx. 30 minutes. Use long tongs to remove from the fire. Check doneness and refold to cook more, if needed. Be careful - they will be hot - and steam will rise when you open the foil. That can burn, so keep it away from your face.

Serve with crusty bread or rolls.

Optional: you can substitute with 1/2 cup of Parmesan cheese, if you like that better.

181

CAMPFIRE BANANA SPLITS

4 kinda green bananas -
   you don't want to use soft bananas
1 bag of chocolate chips
1 bag mini-marshmallows
Optional: salted peanuts
Heavy duty aluminum foil

Take 4 pieces of foil, big enough to hold the meal and allow for folding and wrapping.

Peel each banana and slice long ways. Place two slices on each piece of foil and sprinkle 1/4 cup of chocolate chips and 1/2 cups of mini-marshmallows over the banana slices. Add a sprinkle of peanuts, if you want. Bring up two sides, fold them down, and then fold in the open sides. Place in the campfire for approx. 10 minutes. Use long tongs to remove from the fire. Be careful when opening - they will be hot - and steam will rise when you open the foil. That can burn, so keep it away from your face. Eat with a spoon.

Baked Apples

4 apples, cored and sliced
Brown or white sugar
Cinnamon
Raisins & peanuts
Heavy duty aluminum foil

Take 4 pieces of foil, big enough to hold the meal and allow for folding and wrapping.

Place apple slices on foil. Sprinkle with cinnamon and sugar. Add raisins and nuts, if you want.

Bring up two sides, fold them down, and then fold in the open sides. Place in the campfire for approx. 15 minutes. Use long tongs to remove from the fire. Be careful when opening—they will be hot—and steam will rise when you open the foil. That can burn, so keep it away from your face. Eat with a spoon.

Optional: you can use honey instead of sugar, if you want. It will be juicier, but just as sweet. You can also use peaches or pears.

TOOLS:

> Pot holders that fit on your hands like gloves
> Long handled tongs
> Your mess kit, which includes utensils
> A towel to fold and place on your lap so you can set your meal on it and eat

HERE'S SOMETHING FUN
BUT ONLY WITH ADULTS SUPERVISION.

> Individual camp burners and stoves
> 1 empty and clean tuna fish can (remove the paper label)
> 1 large prepared juice can (see below)
> 1 18" strip of corrugated cardboard, cut the same width of the tuna can.
> Paraffin wax, melted

Take the strip of cardboard and roll it up tight, jelly-roll fashion. Put it inside the tuna can and let it unroll to fill the can. Pour melted wax into the can and fill it to the top. Let the wax harden overnight. This is your burner.

For the stove: to prepare the can, make 2 small openings on one with a can opener that makes triangle holes. Pour out the juice and save for drinking. Remove the paper label and scrub off the glue. Rinse out the can and let it drain. It doesn't have to be totally dry.

On the end without the holes, take a regular can opener and remove the bottom. Save the bottom to use to put out the burning tuna can. Then take metal cutters (have an adult help) and make 2 cuts wide enough for the tuna can and about 4 inches long. Fold the flap up and under to the inside of the can.

To use for cooking: place the can, open side down, on a hard surface like a sidewalk or hard dirt that has all sticks, leaves, pine needles and other things that could burn cleared away. Light the wax in the tuna can and slide the can into the opening of the large can. You can use a stick or a long cooking fork. The can will heat quickly. You can cook on top of the juice can. The small holes will be used for draining liquid or oils.

To extinguish the tuna can, use tongs to pick up the large can and again to place the bottom of the juice can over the flames. Make sure you have pot holders handy, as well. Do not use water to put out the burning wax - it will splatter! If you need to do something more, use dirt. But you won't be able to use the tuna can again if you do.

Things you can cook on your juice can stove
Bacon & eggs
Burgers
Chicken
Hotdogs
Grilled cheese

It takes some experimenting to work with this kind of stove. And you'll need a small amount of oil to keep things from sticking too bad. Campers can also use mess kits, and set our small pans on top of the stove. It's a lot easier to cook that way because it tempers the heat, but try cooking right on the can top, just for the experience.

CREATOR'S NOTES

I am enchanted with the world of Honey Moon, the younger sister of Harry Moon. She is smart and courageous and willing to do anything to help right win out. What a powerhouse.

I wish I had a friend like Honey when I was in school. There is something cool about the way Honey and her friends connect with each other that's very special. When I was Honey's age, I spent most of my time in our family barn taking care of rabbits and didn't hang out with other kids a lot. I think I was always a little bit on the outside.

Maybe that's why I like Honey so much. She lives life with wonderful energy and enthusiasm. She doesn't hesitate to speak her mind. And she demands that adults pay attention to her because more often than not, the girl knows what she is talking about. And she often finds herself getting into all kinds of crazy adventures.

We all need real friends like Honey. Growing up is quite an adventure and living it with girlfriends that you love builds friendships that can last a lifetime. That's the point, I think, of Honey's enchanted world — life is just better when you work it out with friends.

I am happy that you have decided to join me, along with author Regina Jennings, in the enchanted world of Honey Moon. I would love for you to let us know about any fun ideas you have for Honey in her future stories. Visit harrymoon.com and let us know.

See you again in our next visit to the enchanted world of Honey Moon!

MARK ANTHONY POE

189

The Enchanted World of Honey Moon creator Mark Andrew Poe never thought about creating a town where kids battled right and wrong. His dream was to love and care for animals, specifically his friends in the rabbit community.

Along the way, Mark became successful in all sorts of interesting careers. He entered the print and publishing world as a young man and his company did really, really well. Mark also became a popular and nationally sought-after health care advocate for the care and well-being of rabbits.

Years ago, Mark came up with the idea of a story about a young boy with a special connection to a world of magic, all revealed through a remarkable rabbit friend. Mark worked on his idea for several years before building a collaborative creative team to help him bring his idea to life.

Harry Moon was born. The team was thrilled when Mark introduced Harry's enchanting sister, Honey Moon. Boy, did she pack an unexpected punch!

In 2014, Mark began a multi-book project to launch *The Amazing Adventures of Harry Moon* and *The Enchanted World of Honey Moon* into the youth marketplace. Harry and Honey are kids who understand the difference between right and wrong. Kids who tangle with magic and forces unseen in a town where "every day is Halloween night." Today, Mark and the creative team continue to work on the many stories of Harry and Honey and the characters of Sleepy Hollow. He lives in suburban Chicago with his wife and his 25 rabbits.

SUZANNE BROOKS KUHN

Suzanne Brooks Kuhn is a mom and author with a passion for children's stories. Suzanne brings her precocious childhood experiences and sassy storytelling ability to her creative team in weaving the magical stories found in *The Enchanted World of Honey Moon*. Suzanne lives with her husband in an 1800's farmhouse nestled in the countryside of central Virginia.

BE SURE TO READ THE
CONTINUING AND ENCHANTED
ADVENTURES OF HONEY MOON.

HONEY MOON 🌑 BOOK CLUB

Become a member of the
Honey Moon Book Club and receive another
of Honey's adventures every other month
along with a bag full of goodies!

Skip over to www.harrymoon.com
and sign up today.

ALSO IN THE HONEY MOON LIBRARY:

THE
ENCHANTED
WORLD OF
HONEY
MOON

A SCARY LITTLE CHRISTMAS

Suzanne Brooks Kuhn   Created by Mark Andrew Poe

THE
ENCHANTED
WORLD OF
HONEY
MOON

NOT YOUR VALENTINE

Suzanne Brooks Kuhn   Created by Mark Andrew Poe

THE
ENCHANTED
WORLD OF
HONEY
MOON

SHADES AND SHENANIGANS

Suzanne Brooks Kuhn   Created by Mark Andrew Poe

THE
ENCHANTED
WORLD OF
HONEY
MOON

SCARY SMART HOUSE

Suzanne Brooks Kuhn   Created by Mark Andrew Poe

Dear Diary: _____

194

DEAR DIARY

195

Dear Diary: _____

DEAR DIARY

197

Dear Diary: _____

198